Praise for Karen Rivers'

The Healing Time of Hickeys

"This book will have you laughing out loud. Haley is a completely loveable and crazy character. Her quirky thoughts are fun to read and her adventures in dating (or lack of) will have you giggling until your sides ache. It's guaranteed to make you giggle and feel good — what more could you want in a book?" — *Kidzworld*

"Sixteen-year-old Haley Harmony is ... a likeable, grounded soul, despite the fact that she spends an awful lot of time hyperventilating ... A pleasure from start to finish." — *Quill & Quire*

The Cure for Crushes

"I can't help it. I'm a sucker for Bridget Jones and I'm a sucker for Karen Rivers's ongoing series based on the star-crossed life of Haley Harmony. We first met the unfortunately named Harmony (hippie parents, home-schooled, deck stacked against her socially) in *The Healing Time of Hickeys*. It's refreshing that Haley, told through v. funny diary entries, is not entirely likeable; nor are her friends endlessly patient. And without her brother's shoulder to lean on, Haley finds herself alone more this time than last, wondering, like all of us, if she really is capable of happiness and how to make the good hair days outnumber the bad." — *The Georgia Straight*

"We've all had our fair share of red-faced moments, and that's why it's so easy to relate to the accident-prone Haley. Her quirky accidents and comical thoughts are the best part of the book cuz they'll make you laugh until your stomach hurts!" — *Kidzworld*

The Quirky Girls' Guide to Rest Stops and Road Trips
"Fans of the Haley [Andromeda] books (*The Healing Time of Hickeys* and *The Cure for Crushes*) will definitely enjoy the conclusion of the trilogy. Yes, it's chick lit, lite chick lit (is that chick lite???), but it's fun, perfect for a quick read over the holidays, maybe even on a road trip! Buy it for your young Haley wanna-bes, and make sure that you have the two preceding volumes for those who like to read a complete series."
— Joanne Peters, *CM Magazine*

"Teen readers will find Haley's diary filled with countless moments of recognition as Rivers, with spot-on accuracy, captures contemporary teen life." — *Quill & Quire*

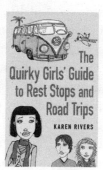

The Healing Time of Hickeys
978-1-55192-600-1
$10.95

The Cure for Crushes
978-1-55192-779-4
$11.95

The Quirky Girls' Guide to Rest Stops and Road Trips
978-1-55192-907-1
$10.95

X in Flight

 in Flight

BOOK ONE

KAREN RIVERS

RAINCOAST BOOKS
www.raincoast.com

Raincoast Books gratefully acknowledges the financial support of the Province of
British Columbia through the BC Arts Council and the Book Publishing Tax
Credit and the Government of Canada through the Canada Council for the Arts,
and the Book Publishing Industry Development Program (BPIDP).

Edited by Colin Thomas
Cover by David Drummond
Interior design by Tannice Goddard

NATIONAL LIBRARY OF CANADA CATALOGUING IN PUBLICATION DATA

Rivers, Karen, 1970–
  X in Flight / Karen Rivers.
ISBN 13: 978-1-55192-982-8
ISBN 10: 1-55192-982-1
  I. Title.
PS8585.I8778X25 2007   JC813'.54   C2007-900492-X

LIBRARY OF CONGRESS CONTROL NUMBER: 2007921214

Raincoast Books   *In the United States:*
9050 Shaughnessy Street   Publishers Group West
Vancouver, British Columbia   1700 Fourth Street
Canada V6P 6E5   Berkeley, California
www.raincoast.com   94710

Printed in Canada by Webcom.

10 9 8 7 6 5 4 3 2 1

For Clayton, my hero

X

1

SO HI. IT'S me. X.

In case you've ever wondered, it's short for *Xenos*. Yeah, I know. Save your breath, I've heard it all before. A Greek name is just the wrong name for a guy who looks like me. It's not much of a name at all, if you ask me, for anyone. Obviously I'm as far from Greek as you can get and still be a part of the same species. I don't know why Deer chose it and she claims she didn't have a big reason; it just struck her as cool at the time. I mostly don't buy that story. I think people have reasons for everything they do. On the other hand, Deer ... well, she's kind of inclined to be random.

Sometimes I think that maybe she's trying to tell me something without actually saying it, because, for some reason, it's against her principles to talk about my father. Like maybe he was Greek. But then again, I doubt it. I mean, unless Greece is full of Africans, it just seems like a pretty unlikely scenario. Look at me. I am 100 percent mulatto: part African-American, black, whatever it's

politically correct to say, and part not. I think people *think*
I know the correct words to use, the right terminology, but
how could I? It's not like every black kid in the world is
born with a handbook of which terms are okay to say and
which aren't. You might be shocked to know that
the NAACP doesn't update us daily on political correctness
via instant message. Not that I care what's "right" or
"wrong." None of it offends me. Except the obvious stuff,
of course. The N-word, for example. I can live without
that.

No one else here can relate to any of this stuff, that's for
sure. Not in this snow white town filled to last-gasping
with people so old their noses touch the ground when they
walk. Old *white* people. They say it's a city for the newly
wed and nearly dead. They should somehow include
"white" in that description, but that would seem to somehow be highlighting race, and race is something no one
ever ever *ever* wants to talk about. Not really. It's like it's
a deep dark scary secret no one wants to reveal. Hey, I
know I'm black. I just think it's weird how people pretend
not to notice. It's bullshit is what it is. It's embarrassing.

You've probably never thought about it at all. Why
would you? You're one of the whitest white people I've
ever seen. So pale it's almost scary, like paper that's never
seen ink, so thin you can see the grain of the table through
it. But in a good way, I mean. In a pretty way. In a way
that makes you seem like you aren't quite real.

Hey, I'll tell you something dumb:

When I was a little kid, I used to think that if I stayed
out in the sun for a long time, I'd fade. Like I was just the
opposite of everyone else — they'd go sun brown, I'd go
sun white. When that didn't work, I thought maybe I

could bleach myself and come out looking like I felt like I should, like everyone else. Stupid, huh? I tried putting my finger in bleach once, held it there for as long as I dared. Good thing it was just my finger. It was a mistake. I was four, okay? I didn't know any better.

My finger turned white-white. Like milk or chalk or bone. Scary white, not living, breathing, flesh-pink white, not even the palest kind of white. I was so, so scared. I thought my finger would die or fall off, and I couldn't even begin to imagine how I'd explain what I'd done. I knew I was in some serious trouble. But it worked out. I don't remember how it happened, but my finger went back to normal.

I guess I am what I am. I can't change myself, not the packaging, anyway. Well, hopefully I'll grow out of the zits, but still. This is it. I don't want to look like everyone else, anyway. I'd rather be different.

I would.

Okay, I wouldn't. But I wish I was the kind of person who did, you know? It sucks to stand out. Sometimes I'd rather just disappear altogether. Yeah. But you know what that's like, I'll bet. I think maybe that's why you and I are ... Well. I think maybe it's why I *like* you. I do. I like you.

That seems like a weird thing to say out loud, or even to type.

Why am I doing this?

Why you?

Why not?

I don't have a lot of other people. I don't have much of a family. Like, a father, like I said. I'm a fatherless son. Sounds poetic, but really it's just shit when it's happening to you, believe me.

Seeing as I'm spilling my guts, I'll tell you something else I'd never really tell you:

I make up what he's like in my head. I call him "Daddy," which is so fucking lame, I can't believe it. I know it, you don't have to tell me. I wouldn't ever tell anyone that I did that. Except you, I guess, if you're reading this. If I knew him, I'm sure I wouldn't call him "Daddy." I'm not six years old, I'm seventeen. I'd probably call him "Dad." Or "Pops." "Father." "Pa."

I just wonder what he was *like*. And it's more than wondering. It's like I *have* to know. I can't stand to not know. It pisses me off is what it does. It makes me *crazy*. Just what he looks like even. Other than his skin colour, which obviously was black. But what does that mean? Black isn't everything. It isn't anything. Not when it comes to telling details about a person. People think it's enough of a description to fill in all the blanks, but it doesn't describe jack all. Anyway, wouldn't it be more accurate to say "brown"? No one is actually black, except in *National Geographic* pictures, countries on the equator and bad cartoons.

What kills me about my dad is ... well, everything. Who the hell was he? Did he read books? Was he an asshole? Did he play golf? Did he sing? Did he wear good jeans? Like, *anything*. It makes me mad not to know. It makes me feel like I'm raging inside, like I'll never be quite okay because I'm only half myself. And anyway, why did he choose Deer? And why did she choose him? Was it a party? Was everyone just too drunk to care?

That's what I figure, that they were drunk. Or stoned. Or both. Wasted. I was the big, fat, blurry hangover of an accident in their freewheeling lives.

I wonder if she told him, and if she did, if he cared.

I wonder why she didn't just have an abortion and get rid of me.

I wonder if she even knew who the father was when she found out she was pregnant.

Oh, fuck that. I don't want to know. I do. But I don't. And she'll never tell, it's like she thinks it's none of my business and I can't make her see it any other way. It makes me want to *cry*. Fuck. How would you feel if all you knew of your daddy was his skin colour and the texture of his hair?

I have a 'fro. I guess you wouldn't know because I keep it clipped so short that it's just a shadow-cap on my skull. Dark on dark. Deer says I come by my skin tone from my Indian grandmother. (Thinking about her makes me think of that popsicle-stick longhouse we had to build in the fifth grade, remember? Man, I loved that thing. I thought it was the bomb. It was probably crap, but I worked on it for days.) Grandma was Haida, so her skin was tan, her hair long and dark. But seriously, it still doesn't add up. I'm ten times as dark as my mum is — full on brown metallic chocolate WITH AN AFRO. There's no WAY, I tell her. None.

And she shrugs and says, You're beautiful, what does it matter?

Which is great, but it doesn't change the fact that she's full of lies. I'll never get the truth from her. I guess she thinks she's protecting me or some crap like that, when all she's doing is hurting me by hiding all the stuff that matters, all the stuff that matters to *me*. She just doesn't get it.

Besides, I'm not beautiful.

I'm as ugly as can be, inside and out. Tall and knobby kneed, with arms that don't fit in any shirt or sweater I've ever owned. Bones pushing through all over like they're trying to get out. A mouth full of white teeth that should probably be behind braces, which we can't afford, overlapping each other like crooked pickets on a rotting fence. Freckles that look like zits. Zits that look like zits. If this is beauty, someone (God, I guess) has a pretty bad sense of humour.

And he must like zits.

Zitty Xenos, that's me. I bet the Greeks spell zit with an X. Xit.

Even Deer calls me "X," and I call her "Deer." Obviously. My mother, that is. That's "Deer." Not "dear." Short for "Running Deer," which isn't *her* name, either. I made it up. Nice, huh? She thought it was funny and it stuck, when really it was just a dumb joke. Totally not in good taste, but who decides what's good taste, anyway?

It's probably all in that handbook.

Whatever. It's all love, right? You dish it out in ways that people understand.

My little tiny brother Mutt (yes, that's his real name, another long story that maybe I'll tell you later), he calls me Eggs, but that's because he's only three. He still talks like a baby. He can't get his three-year-old mouth around the letter X. Eks. Eggs. See?

Oh, man. I can't believe you're still reading. If you are, that is.

I just, well ... I thought I should tell you something about me, but it turns out that, apart from the surface stuff, the obvious, I don't know what to say or how to say it. I may as well have just described my *room*. Or my shoes, my ugly beat-up Adidas with the orange, red and yellow stripes. Or the old red T-shirt I'm wearing right now, picture of Fidel Castro on the front, hole under the sleeve, not exactly smelling fresh. Or something else that doesn't matter, like my pilled-up, torn, blue plaid flannel sheets.

It's harder than I thought it would be just to get started. To not sound like such an asshole. It's like having a conversation no one can hear; the tone's all wrong. Like when you say something out loud to yourself and then you feel like a crazy jerk and think, "What if someone heard me? What if they caught me? What if they think I'm nuts?" It's like that. I'm talking, no one's listening, and I don't know where to stop or start or even why I'm doing it.

The punchline is that none of this is the real story. Who gives a crap about my name, anyway? There really IS a story and what I've told you is nothing to do with it.

I guess I believe you need to know who I think I am so you can understand the rest. Remember a few months back when we had to write that essay, "Who Are You?", for English? I should have just given you my copy of that; it was a lot of the same garbage. My name. My skin colour. A bunch of stuff I was thinking about race, stuff I don't usually talk about. Deep stuff. I left out the personal things, though. Some things are just no one's business.

I left out the big things.

The important things.

The things that mean something.

The things I want to tell you.

Hey, if you figure out what any of this means, tell me. Seriously.

Ready for the punchline?

You think you are, but you aren't. I sure wasn't. But I've got to tell you. I've got to tell someone, and I picked you. Because it has something to do with you. Or maybe I just want it to. It did, the first time.

Here it is:

I can *fly*.

It's true. And when I say "fly," I don't mean, like, *metaphorically*. Or in a plane or a glider or a helicopter or anything like that. I sure don't mean on my feet either.

I was never the best runner.

And I've never been on a plane, but I imagine it doesn't feel anything like this.

This is something else. It's comic book stuff. Except not. It's not heroic. It's just ... there. There doesn't seem to be a point to it. Anyway, if I was going to pick a super-hero quality, I would have chosen to be fast or ripped or invisible or a mind reader or all those things. Brave. So strong I could lift cars. Something macho. But nope, that's not what I got. I got "flying." Funny thing, really. I mean, Superman was always my least favourite character.

At first I was scared. *Really* scared, not only because it was so fucking weird, but because I'm terrified of heights. So terrified that the adrenalin feels like too much, so it feels like your skin might break apart from your body, and you might just turn into liquid, evaporating into nothingness.

Now? Now it's just what it is. Part of me.

If you aren't going to believe any of this, then you should just stop reading right now. Seriously. I know it doesn't make sense, that it sounds insane. I get that it sounds like a lie. I understand if you're freaking out.

One thing I've figured out recently is that nobody likes

to think that completely unbelievable things happen every day. Just like that, out of the blue. *Ka-pow*, like they say in the cartoons. One day, you're just a kid — a kid with a talent for golf and that's about it, living in a trailer that pretends to be a house in a field full of cows and stray golf balls with your hippie mother and three-year-old brother who likes to pretend he's a girl or a dog or a fish or a rock star. And the next day — like your life isn't already messed up enough — the next day, you can fly.

I'm tripping over myself to tell this right and it's not working, is it? I feel like I've started in the middle and gone on too long.

I could have written, "Dear Ruby, I can fly. How are you?" but I'll never give this to you, so who cares? I don't even *know* you, except that I know who you are. I feel this *connection* to you, but that sounds too stupid to say out loud, so I won't. It doesn't matter to me. Read it. Don't read it. I like you anyway. Dumb, right? I can't help it. You're something different. You're ... I don't know. I don't know why I'm trying to convince you. I guess it's because you don't like yourself.

I can tell.

I'm right, right?

Anyway, it doesn't matter. I just wanted to get this down before I go crazy trying to figure it out some other way.

I wish I was a great writer because this would some-how, some way, make an amazing story. Maybe even a movie. I should pay more attention in English class instead of just jackassing around with my boys or staring out the window and counting down the minutes 'til I can get out. 'Til I can breathe. Staring at the back of your neck at the fine line of hair that never quite makes it into your ponytail.

Sorry. I guess I sound like a stalker or something. Psycho. I'm not. I swear it. It's not like I'm wanting to get *with* you, I just feel like you and me — we're different, like you and me maybe know stuff that other people don't. I can fly, why can't you have some kind of crazy-weird thing, too?

Besides, I have a girlfriend. I *did* have a girlfriend. I have a sometimes-girlfriend. I have Cat.

It's not about that. It's really not. I hope I'm not scaring you.

Look, I feel like I've missed some important details. About me. About Deer. I guess I have "issues." I hate that word, but what else is there?

It goes all the way back to when I was born. It was just a straight up born-in-the-hospital-no-story-here kind of bullshit, which is only worth mentioning because if Deer had been as bad as she is now I would have been born in a wading pool in some hippies' basement. The part building up to it was probably more interesting, like when Deer joined a cult (it wasn't a cult, she says repeatedly, it was just a group of people working together to make the world a better place) and travelled around the world, apparently oblivious to the fact that it's easy to get pregnant when you're not using any kind of protection and you're sleeping with everyone you meet.

That's a terrific thing to know about your mother. Really healthy. No wonder I'm so messed up.

I know about your mother, by the way. Everyone knows. About the fire. About how she threw you off the balcony and about how she died. That's ... I don't know how to say it. I mean, obviously it sucks. But it's more than that. It's the worst thing. It sort of ... well, it makes me think that maybe I'm right about you. Like maybe something happened to you that day to make you ... special. Somehow. I don't know. I just hope it did.

At least ... anyway. Whatever. I'm sorry about your mother. I hope you have other people who fill you up.

I don't. I mean, other than Deer and Mutt, there's no one. Deer was an only child. Her mother is dead, died before I can remember. And her dad ... well, her dad. He was like her best friend, but when she had a black baby (that would be me), he walked out of the hospital and never came back. He's what we call a "bigot." Deer never mentions him. Not much, anyway. There are pictures of him, though. White guy. Funny thing that he could marry a First Nations woman and still be prejudiced against African-Americans, but maybe bigots pick and choose.

People let you down. That's the lesson, right? Your whole life long, probably, people who you think will always be there are bailing out.

It's dark outside. So dark. Winter. Dark and still. I never thought I'd say it, but I miss the crickets and frogs that most of the year are so unfuckinbelievably noisy it's like they're living in my head. Sometimes I hate noise. In the spring and summer, I stuff Kleenex in my ears but it doesn't help at all, it's still all chirp chirp chirpy. But now it's completely silent. I wish I had an iPod so I could block out all that nothingness. The only thing I can hear is Mutt breathing his wet, kid breathing in the bunk under mine. Seventeen years old and sharing a bunk bed with my three-year-old brother. Nice, huh?

Shut up, Mutty, I say out loud. Nicely, but still.

Mmmf, he says in his sleep, stuffing his thumb in his mouth, slurping away on it like it's a root beer popsicle.

I sketch a car I'll never be able to afford in the edge of my notebook by the light of the clip-on lamp. I'm not supposed to be writing letters (or whatever this is) that I'll never send. I should be doing homework. Math. In the bad light, the numbers are even harder to make any sense of. This stupid lamp is old and wrecked and gets brighter and dimmer, depending on the angle I prop it at with my shoulder. The light bulb burns my skin.

I have to tell you something else that's important.

Sometimes I hate myself. I want to take this pen and drive it through the palm of my hand. Why?

I don't know.

I'm no one special.

I'm special because I can fly.

Or maybe I can fly because I'm special.

I never thought of it like that. I like it better that way around. Although it doesn't make much sense because, let's face it, I'm really not special at all. Although maybe I'm *supposed* to be.

I'm just X.

This is who I am.

CAT

2

CAT FLIPS THROUGH a mess of books that she's grabbed randomly from her sister's alphabetically arranged shelf. She doesn't know what she's looking for, and it doesn't much matter. And because it doesn't matter, she knows she'll find it. It could be anything. She opens covers. She feels the pages. She looks at the author bios on the back. Drops them onto the floor, gets up to reach for more.

Her sister, Mira, isn't home. She's at one of her millions of "meetings." Cat lumps them all together as one category: Overachievers Anonymous. It doesn't matter whether it's Save the Environment or Amnesty International or Students Against Drunk Driving. Whatever it is, it all adds up to the same thing. Too much.

Mira's bed is made perfectly. Sheets so tight they practically propel Cat back up again when she throws herself down onto them. She bounces hard, on her feet, jumping like a kid. Jumping until she's out of breath. Jumping until the bed has softened up. Messed into comfort. She stops bouncing and starts reading randomly from a stack of books she's dropped in a heap on the floor. Poetry.

Gross.

She hates poetry. Especially *pretty* poetry. Robert Frost. Emily Dickinson. Yawn.

What she hates more, though, is asinine questions like "Who Are You?" that have to be answered in essay form, double-spaced, in black type (Times New Roman or Arial only). She decided right away that she wouldn't write a stupid essay. She'd do something even more abhorrently ridiculous. She'd answer the question with a poem.

Originally, she planned to write her own, but she tried for about an hour and her verse was shit and she was too tired to try again. To tell the truth, she'd ended up toggling over to the internet and talking in a chat room about body piercings for forty-five minutes. By the time she was done with that, the computer was starting to give her a headache. All those pixels bouncing off her brain. To make matters worse, she'd read about how some girl her age had a belly-button ring that got infected and somehow the infection got into her blood and she croaked. Probably an urban myth, but it still made her feel funny. Light-headed. Dizzy.

Cat fingers her belly-button ring. It's a small hoop with a scorpion hanging from it, a tiny diamond in its pincer grasp. The scorpion gets caught on the waistband of her jeans sometimes and makes her hair stand up, like hearing nails on a chalkboard or biting tinfoil. That squeamish squirm that seems to form in your pores and make your skin shift. It doesn't bother her though. The pinching feeling reminds her to breathe.

None of Mira's parts are pierced. Well, except her ears.

Mira, Cat drawls, lying on Mira's bed with her head on Mira's pillow, staring at Mira's things. Mira, Mira, Mira. I admire ya, Mira, she says.

Cat doesn't understand how she and Mira could look so alike and be so different on the inside. It's like Mira is lit by an internal flame of goodness and she's ignited by coal tar or worse. She imagines that even Mira's organs are all clean and tagged and orderly, whereas her own are probably all blackened at the edges from smoking and are sloppily stuffed into basically the right places well enough to function, but not properly. Not quite right.

If Mira had to write an essay about herself, it would be twenty tidy pages long and full of footnotes and quotes, in the correct font, clean and intelligent. She'd know how to do it right without asking anyone, without struggling for one second, without first procrastinating for four hours. Cat's will likely be stained or torn by the time she gets it to the teacher. Something always happens. Something dirties it all up.

Mira, Mira, blah, blah, blah, thinks Cat, closing her eyes. She wants to scream or fall asleep or both. She's tired. The red pattern of her eyelids against the light makes her think of sea creatures or ocean plants. Insomnia keeps her awake every night. Last night, she lay in bed, and, unable to stop her brain from unfurling all her waking thoughts, she thought about X. She had to fight the urge to get out of bed, walk to his house barefoot, yell at him. For what? She doesn't know why she feels so pissed off when she thinks of him, so full of self-loathing, so inclined to punch her fist into the glass on Mira's white, little-girl dressing table. When she thinks about herself and X, thinks about them together, she bubbles over with something an awful lot like rage. Slumps into self-doubt. Feels incandescently *furious*. That's the stuff that usually keeps her awake, eyes forced open by her racing heart, staring at the shadows and the lights from passing cars sliding down the wall behind her bed.

X is her boyfriend. *Boyfriend*. Who says that word anymore? It sounds wrong. He's her *boy*. That's more often what she calls him. Her boy. Hers.

She's *happy*.

He's gorgeous, freakishly beautifully made. Perfect. Like a male model, he's lanky and angular. Dark skin, fierce blue eyes, shaved smooth head. Cheekbones like blades. She wants to take photos of him, capture him in the lens, blur his outline, highlight his eyes. She wants to *catch* him in her camera and keep him, but for some reason, when she tries, she gets shy. She misses the shot. She fucks it up.

She should just concentrate on taking weird pictures of inanimate junk instead. That's her calling. Her "art." Pictures of zippers. Piercings. Drops of water sliding off wire fences. Garbage spilling out of cans. Stuff like that. Ugly pretty. Pretty ugly.

What it comes down to is that she can't believe that X chose her in the first place, that they've been together for two years. Who would *choose* her? She has nothing to offer. She isn't smart or hot or pretty or funny or even really very much fun. Her own father says she's ugly. Okay, he says her piercings are ugly, but her piercings are as much *her* as anything else is. She keeps thinking that X will realize his mistake, will dump her suddenly and hurtfully, and she'll be caught off guard, off balance. She'll fall. She'd hate that. So instead, her brain takes over and forces her to imagine a film reel of what's probably going to happen. To guess what he must be thinking. She practises in her head for the ending. It makes her ache. It makes her hate him enough to make herself feel okay.

From the other room, she can hear the rise and fall of a too-boisterous-to-be-meaningful conversation. Her mum on the phone, yammering away, her voice like bells or cymbals. Bam bam bam-ditty-bam. Clang clang. Cat can hear threads of the conversation, although it is just far enough away that she has to strain to listen, to weave it back together. She hears the words "very proud" and deflates. Her mum is bragging again to someone on the phone about Mira. Must be. Their parents are so proud of Mira that their eyes shine like mirrors when she comes into the room, always with some big announcement. Some great thing she's done. Some kid she's saved from a burning building or some charity she's given a fortune to in pennies collected in a jar. Something she's won or achieved or been recognized for. Cat's bile rises in her throat. It's as though she, Cat, doesn't even exist.

I need to use the phone, Ma, she screams.

Though she doesn't. And even if she did, she has her own cell phone, makes all her calls on that for privacy.

For good measure, she picks up the extension in Mira's room, sighs noisily into the receiver, then slams it down. This won't make her mother hang up; she knows it won't. But it will bug her, and that's enough. Her mother talks on the phone about ten hours a day, unless she's out selling makeup to old people. Cat's mother's Avon route involves five local "retirement homes," which Cat calls "Death's Waiting Rooms." She went with her mother once and nearly killed herself, it was so depressing. Old people sitting around with vacant expressions on their faces and their teeth in jars beside them, spending the money they probably spent their whole lives saving on Rabid Raspberry Lip Smackers and Sparkling Wine nail polish. And the smell!

The smell.

Cat gets dizzy thinking about it. Can't breathe. Feels like she's gagging on mothballs. The stench was unforgettable, saturating: cleaners and body waste and something worse. Like the smell of death itself. It was the most hideous-smelling experience of her life.

Mira, of course, *loved* it. She still, even now, goes once a week to play Scrabble with the old bats. She reads them poetry and calls it a "workshop" when really it's more like storytime at a kindergarten. What a suckhole. Cat can't believe that she's related to such a simp. She kicks at Mira's comforter until she's made even more of a nest, ignoring the fact that some old caked mud from her boots clumps off onto Mira's white pillow. She forces herself to read another poem from another book. It sucks. It rhymes and it's cheerful, like some kind of hideous birthday card featuring a dew-spattered rosebud. Terrible. It reads like song lyrics for some kind of feel-good, up-with-people choir.

Cat can't sing, but wishes she could. Not in a choir, not that kind of singing, but fronting a band of edgy, strung-out rockers. Something noisy and pissed off. With screaming. With *rage*. She looks like that kind of singer. People see her barbell and her belly-button ring and her haircut and her clothes and think she is one. Of course, she muses, *people* don't know shit about anything. People *suck*. And just because you look a certain way means jack all. Look at X. He's a *golfer*. He looks too cut and cool and edged out to be a golfer. Way too *alternative*. But inside, he's just a preppy white guy in an argyle cardigan and knickers, perfecting his putt.

Cat hates golf.

But she loves X. She really does love him. *Love*. The word makes her puke, but it doesn't make her feelings less real. And because she loves X, sometimes she carries his bag when he plays in tournaments. She even takes the piercings out of her face because, for some reason, golf courses get to dictate whether or not you have a one-inch piece of metal above your eye. Uptight bastards. She hates golf courses, golf clubs and golf pros. And X's golf bag, which weighs about two hundred pounds, but which she carries without complaining. Cat is nothing if not tough. Nothing if not strong. While Mira is trouncing around the town doing good deeds and learning things that her mum can brag about later, Cat is usually at the gym or at the pool. Lifting weights, swimming, running. She has tons of energy. Sometimes, she has so much excess energy she wouldn't be surprised if she just left the ground altogether one day. It's like she's buzzing. Constantly. That's part of the reason for the pot she smokes daily, she rationalizes. It's the only thing that makes the buzzing stop.

Speaking of pot, she's been staring at the same page for at least twenty minutes. The last hit was too much. Mira's room smells so much like *Mira* that it's making Cat's head ache and her throat clench. It's a soapy, clean, papery smell. Soft. She hangs over the edge of Mira's bed and looks underneath, hoping to find something that would incriminate her sister, make her seem less perfect. A diary or porn or an empty bottle of JD or even a candy wrapper. Nothing. She sighs, still upside down, the blood pulsing behind her eyes. There aren't even any dustballs. Clean, sunny, bright Mira. Well, fuck, she thinks, sitting up so fast her head feels light and fluffy, like a dandelion gone to seed. She closes her eyes.

Good thing my parents had Mira or they'd be really sad to have just been stuck with me, she thinks.

Back up on the bed, which is now in complete shambles, Cat flexes herself into a back bend and, upside down, observes the Greenpeace poster that Mira has over her headboard. She wonders whether Mira ever wants to rip that thing down and become someone else. Replace it with something ugly, something dark. Experimentally, she flexes, and then pushes off with her feet, idly wondering whether she's still strong enough to get up onto her hands from this position.

She isn't.

Her feet hit the poster — does it tear? — and she crashes onto the floor, half-laughing, half-hurt.

What are you DOING up there? her father yells.

NOTHING, she screams back.

Pretty noisy for NOTHING, he shouts.

I'm doing my HOMEWORK, she says.

Try to do it more quietly, he says from the doorway.

Okay, she says.

He stares at her for a second. His lip curls as if he's about to say something, then he shakes his head. Hard. Like there is water he's trying to dislodge from his ear.

And try to do it in your own room, he says.

Yeah, she says.

Her own room is a pit. There are clothes everywhere — and CDs and papers and ... junk. Mira's room is nicer. Well, mostly because it's clean.

And clean up your sister's room before you leave it, he says.

She can hear his heavy footsteps on the stairs. Clomp, clomp, clomp.

Hey, Dad, she wants to yell. Are you HAPPY? Is this the life you wanted?

But she doesn't. She gets up and tugs Mira's comforter back into some semblance of "flat." Grabs yet another book from the now half-empty shelf and flips it open, tears out a page. There, she thinks. *This* page of *this* book will be my answer to "Who Are You?"

Why not?

Cat slams back into her own room, which stinks like stale cigarettes and laundry and something rotting, and types the poem into her computer, changing a few words just to make it less like cheating and more true. For a second, she thinks that maybe she should trash this idea and, instead, type out the lyrics for that old Police song that her mum loves so much. She thinks it's called "Don't Stand So Close to Me" or some crap like that. Then the teacher would know that *she* knows that he's hot for her. Staring at her boobs all class. Trying to meet her eye. Blushing when she stares him down. Creep. She's ON to him. She *knows*.

Nah.

She sticks with the poem. Prints it out with her name at the top, all in capital letters in some fancy-ass font she picked off the list just to piss him off. Done, she grins. She glares at the phone, willing it to ring. She hasn't talked to X all day.

Call me, she says in her head. Call me call me call me call me.

The phone doesn't ring.

Come on, come on, come on.

She's hungry. She wants ice cream. Mint chocolate chip.
If he calls, she can talk him into it. She can talk him into
anything, she figures. Come on, she croons to the phone.
Come onnnnn.

She could call him, but she won't. That's not her style.
Instead, she paces around. Dances a bit. Turns on some
music and really dances, bashing into the wall, knocking
over an empty goldfish bowl in which she'd been keeping
interesting junk she found on the street: bottle caps and
broken things. It feels so goooood to dance hard, rubbish
digging into her through the soles of her boots. She dances
until her dad bashes on the ceiling downstairs so loudly
she can feel it in her feet.

She flips him off, even though he can't see her. Then
does the same to her quiet cell phone. Fuck you, she says,
fuck you fuck YOU. She settles herself back down in front
of the computer, sweaty and breathing hard. There's a
website she heard of that shows you how to do prison tat-
toos with regular pen ink. She's thinking of making a
tattoo of an X on her upper arm. She's drawn it out
already. It's not just an X, it's fancy. Kind of Celtic, and
kind of tribal. It's going to rule, she thinks. She just has to
convince someone to help her so that it's not all crooked.

Mira'll do it, she figures. She just has to find some way
to bribe her, or to blackmail her into not telling their mum
and dad.

Get off the PHONE, Mum, she screams. I need to make
a call, and my phone is DEAD!

Then she settles into her internet daze, flipping from
one page to the next until she finds exactly what she's
looking for.

Ruby

3

YOU SIT AT the dining room table. The computer screen is blank. Obviously. In front of you, there is a glass buffet full of different glasses that the housekeeper keeps polished and glittering in spite of the fact that only one or two have ever been used. They're pretty, the light bouncing off them like water. It moves in a way that gives you vertigo. You watch until you realize the illusion of movement is just your shadow, shifting as you turn.

The clock in the living room ticks. It's a cuckoo clock, which is incongruous in this otherwise angular glass and chrome setting. The little wooden bird lurches out and shrieks on the hour. It makes you jump every single time.

The TV is on with no sound, throwing colours in radiant patterns onto the highly polished black enamel floor. In the silence, you can hear that you are alone. The air moves differently — cooler and scentless and somehow less friendly — when your father isn't home. He isn't home very much, not lately. He's very busy! He's in demand!

You can't imagine what it must be like to be so popular, so wanted. Just last week, he was interviewed on national TV, on some morning news show that apparently everyone in the world sees. People keep saying, "I saw your dad ..." You are already getting used to nodding, saying "thank you," even though you're not sure why you should be grateful. It's nothing to do with you. Your father has written a book that at this exact moment is number four on the *New York Times* bestseller list. A funny, analytical book (that's what the reviews say) about being a single father and about being a shrink and about a whole bunch of other things too personal to even contemplate. In a way — in most ways — the book is pretty much completely about you, which is why you'd rather stick a fork in your eye than actually read it. The cover is bad enough: a girl who looks nothing like you stares at a candle flame, the flame itself reflecting in the girl's eye like in that old Drew Barrymore movie about the kid who lit things on fire with a glance.

On the other hand, you wish you could hand the book in to your teacher, in place of answering this impossible essay question: "Who Are You?" It's a sentence sort of answer, not even a paragraph. Not even an interesting sentence.

You type your name, which is all that springs to mind.

Ruby. I am Ruby.

That's all you have.

You lean your face close to the glass tabletop and exhale. You make a perfect fingerprint with your index finger in the fog of your breath. If you were braver, you would take a picture of *that* and hand it in as your essay. Your fingerprint on the glass is as much "you" as anything else is. Besides, you feel like this is one of those artsy philosophical kinds of questions that you should be able to answer in a "different" way. Turn the project into something else. If you were a teacher, you'd hand your students the question and tell them they could answer any way they wanted to, *except* by writing an essay. An essay is no way to answer that question for real. Anything you write down is going to sound stilted and dumb and clichéd and will also be full of lies.

Of course, lies tell as much about a person as the truth does.

Still, you want to do something different. A photo could be an answer, but you don't have a camera. A sculpture. A tower made of popsicle sticks or a collage of books you've read, movies you've seen, music you've heard, people you've met. A painting of yourself in the future. You imagine you could do something really wild, like cut off all your hair and mould it somehow into a face and hand THAT in. That would get everyone's attention.

But that isn't you. Not really. Besides, it all sounds like too much work.

You type a line of As and then a line of Bs.

I am a girl, you type slowly, dragging your fingers along the keyboard so that the sentence looks more like Io am, as girlk. And then you delete it, using the backspace key, one letter at a time. Tap-tap-tap.

Which leaves you where you started. You backspace further, until you have just your name. Ruby.

This super *sucks*, you say out loud. Why does it have to be so stupid and so hard?

It feels dumb to talk when no one is there to listen. It makes you feel loopy, like you're drunk or something. Not that you'd know, having never been drunk.

You write, My name is Ruby and I am drunk.

You go back and change "am" to "feel." You don't want the teacher turning you in to the counsellor for having a drinking problem or "suspected drinking problem" or anything equally embarrassing.

What does "drunk" feel like, anyway? You've seen drunk people, you know what they are all about. Well, from a distance, anyway. Up close, you've only really seen Joey Ticcato drunk. When he's drunk, he likes to call you. To see you. Which is easy enough because he lives downstairs, but still it always makes you feel embarrassed. You don't know what it means or what he wants. If you had a close girlfriend, you're sure you would sit around for hours analyzing what he said and did, the way he looked at you or didn't.

Sometimes you want to scream at him, Do you SEE me? What do you WANT?

Other times, most of the time, you're just happy he wants to be around you. You listen while he talks. And talks and talks. Sometimes it makes sense, sometimes it doesn't. You watch him carefully, the way his hand sometimes drifts toward yours and then stops, like one magnet being pushed by another of opposite polarity. When he's talking about something that's really important to him, like a poem he's writing, lyrics he's trying to work out, his blue eyes flare up so brightly they are like the Earth seen from space, a colour that can't exist but does.

This is what's important: this strange need that you fill for him, even when you don't really want to be there. Even when the smell of him makes you gag and when his stories make you cringe.

The downside is that usually, if he's drunk enough to need to see you, he's drunk enough to throw up. Once, lurching, he leaned in (you thought for one heart-stopping moment that he was going to kiss you, you could feel and smell his alcohol-hot breath) and tumbled past you, vomiting like he'd turn inside out. You didn't know what to do. So you patted his back until he jerked out from under your hand, mumbling, Leave me alone, just go away. So you did, face burning, like you'd done something humiliating when really, if you think about it, it's Joey who should have been embarrassed, Joey who should have run away and not looked back.

In any event, drinking doesn't appeal to you. The drunk rambling: who would listen to YOU? The throwing up that seems inevitable; every party you've ever been to has ended with someone's head in the sink, someone puking uncontrollably into the shrubbery on the front walk, someone crying in the bathroom, dry-heaving into the shower stall.

So from where you're sitting, being drunk is as bad as food poisoning with a bunch of embarrassing acting out first. Being drunk makes you either cry and want to die or fall in love with *everyone*. Makes you dance and tell lies and embarrass yourself.

You delete the part about feeling drunk. You change it to I feel crazy, which is infinitely more honest.

This reminds you of a song that you used to sing when you were little. It started with "I am slowly going crazy," which was followed by a jumble of numbers. You try to remember it, but you can't get all the words. The tune sticks in your head, and you close your eyes and shake your head as though you could dislodge it that way.

Joey would remember. He keeps all that kind of stuff, stuff from when you were little kids. He remembers every detail. You'd think with all the drinking and puking, he'd kill some brain cells, but no, it's all still in there. Somehow.

I am slowly going ...

You wish you *were* crazy. Sometimes. Like, controllably crazy, not out-of-control psych-patient crazy. Sometimes, you hope you are. That would give your father something shrink-like to work on that he can actually fix. You think he would be proud if he could fix you. He always seems disappointed that you aren't particularly obviously broken. You're a *teenager*. An *adolescent*. You're supposed to do something outlandish, something *wild*. Sometimes he hints to you as to how you should behave such that he can discipline you (or "help" you) appropriately. You know that you are supposed to be different during this time. Difficult. Hard to get along with. You are supposed to sneak around getting drunk and acting silly. You are supposed to have an inappropriate boyfriend whom you do dumb things with. You are supposed to accidentally get pregnant or arrested or, better yet, both. Imagine the possibilities! He could write a whole series of wildly successful books about your antics.

If only you performed.

You delete again — tap-tap-tap — and you start over.

My name is Ruby, you write. But that is not who I am. Sometimes I feel like I wander far away from myself and I only come back accidentally.

You sit back and look at what you've written, which is true, but it really does sound weird and off-putting, so you delete again. The things you've deleted are probably more meaningful than what you'll eventually write. You know your teacher is not looking for much more than a description. Hair colour, height, weight, hobbies, favourite books, movies, music. Something boring. Something safe. Yet you can't bring yourself to type that information.

This particular teacher, you suspect, will think that he knows the class soooo intimately after reading these self-descriptions, especially if you give him more than he bargained for. You want to make him feel like he's so radically reaching deeply inside everyone to find that precious golden nugget of truth. You want to do this, but in a way that somehow gives you the last laugh. Besides which, you can pretty much accurately guess that really he wants to know only about one person and has assigned the entire class this project to get the one answer. This person that he wants to know about is Cat, whom you've seen him staring at while you are doing "quiet work." Most of his class is "quiet work." Most of his time is spent staring. You wonder what he would say if you turned in a paper that said, "My name is Ruby. PS I know about your stupid crush on Cat." But there is nothing to know. Probably. And if there is, what do you care?

You think that Cat is oblivious to the staring because she is a girl who is stared at all the time, wherever she goes. The opposite of you in almost every way. She's pierced and noisy. Colourful and jarring. She makes you look. She *dares* you to look. Her bracelets slam together like screen doors. Looking at her makes you flinch. She hurts your ears. Your eyes. She's too much on the surface for you. You think she's probably really afraid of something and putting up a false front. Or that's what your dad would say, you're sure of it. Frankly, your dad would probably kill to have a daughter like her. Such a project! You feel

sorry for your dad that he got you instead: quiet, depend-
able, plodding you. He'd do better with in-your-face Cat,
out there getting the attention that she craves. Scaring
people with her bravado. Wanting to sit next to him on TV
shows, laughing or screaming or raging at all the witty
anecdotes about herself in a way that you never ever ever
could.

You just aren't like that.

You are invisible.

That's the truth. Nothing has anything to do with you.
Not really. Not even the book. Although each time you
see that cover advertised on the side of a bus or in a
magazine, your cringe is so all-encompassing that you feel
like you're collapsing into yourself, shrivelling from
humiliation like a slug that's been sprinkled with salt.

My name is Ruby, you type for the tenth time. And I am
invisible. Then you change it to I want to be invisible. Then
you change it back.

This is hard, you say out loud to the TV, which is showing a Tampax ad that is populated by the shrieking kind of
pretty, happy girls that you would rather be than yourself.
The kind of girls that actually, come to think of it, don't
really exist.

Ruby, you type.

Ruby, Ruby, Ruby. "Ruby" is one of those names that,
after you say it over and over again in your head, starts to
sound like nonsense. Like a word that you might have
made up. A word like "phlegm" or "flesh" or "gullet."

You stare fiercely at the screen until you start to see
the floaters in your eyes more clearly than you can see the
words. Your essay is shaping up (if you can call one
sentence "shaping up") to be just like you — way more

serious than you mean to be. You were sort of kidding when you wrote the line about being invisible. And sort of not. But that sarcastic, snappy tone you meant it in isn't there. On the screen, in black and white, it looks like the kind of cry for help that would make your father crazy with joy. He could cure that!

The phone rings. It's set to ring with "Ode to Joy" or some other classical junk you should know, but don't. All those years of music lessons, and you can't even name the ring tone. The chiming and beeping of it is too much sound, the jangle of it makes your heart pound somewhere up near your throat. You don't answer it. You hardly ever answer the phone. You have your own cell phone, and anyone you want to talk to will call you on that number. You can predict with 100 percent accuracy that the person calling is someone who is currently dating your dad, is wanting to date your dad or used to date your dad. The machine picks up and you hear your Auntie A. leaving a long message.

You have about twenty "aunts" who aren't actually related to you. "Aunt" is the title given — for reasons you never understood — by your dad to the wannabes. If they get serious enough, that is. It's something they earn by sticking around for a year or more. Like a badge. Auntie A. was your father's girlfriend from when you were four until you were eight. She says you are like a daughter to her. That's pretty weird, you think, because you feel next to nothing for her. Except sort of sympathetic. Your dad has moved on from her brunette, clean-skinned wholesome type to a more expensive-looking, large-breasted, shiny-skinned, robotic, bottle-blonde type. Unless Auntie A. hits a plastic surgeon and a hairdresser, she has no hope.

Besides, the job is temporarily filled, or so your dad says. And he's excited about it, which is too nauseating to contemplate. This newest contender is some slut named Cassidy, whom you've never met. It doesn't matter though, it's just a matter of time. She'll likely look and act exactly like an overinflated Barbie, as your father's taste is moving increasingly and horrifyingly in that direction. The last one, Gina, had skin so smooth and shiny it looked as though it had been made from melted wax. She practically smelled like plastic. Come to think of it, Gina didn't want to be an "auntie." She wanted you to not exist at all. This is another disturbing aspect of the trend: the bigger the boobs, the blonder the hair, the less YOU seem to matter at all.

The ones who wanted to befriend you were almost better than Gina and her cold shoulder, her way of looking directly through you as though you didn't even register.

You go to the kitchen and pour a glass of water and add plenty of ice, mostly because you like the icemaker in the freezer. When you were little, you used to fill buckets with the ice. Empty ice cream buckets, empty margarine tubs, whatever. The ice springing from its mysterious source never ran out. It was endless. You dumped it all into the tub and stuck your feet in it until they hurt and turned red and then bluish-purple and then stopped hurting. You poked your mottled flesh to make white prints on your skin. For a while your next door neighbours were a family from Japan, and the daughter, Yuki, would come over and you'd both stick your feet in ice together. This was when you were around six. When you think about it now, it seems incredibly weird that two six-year-olds were even allowed to do this. What if you had gotten frostbite?

Then what? Nice responsible parenting, Dad, you think bitterly. Just terrific.

Now you drink the water slowly, crunching your ice cubes. You can't drink water fast. If you have to swallow quickly, you always feel like you're drowning. The crunching of the ice hurts your teeth and sounds too loud in the empty apartment. You make more noise on purpose, just to create a commotion. All your actions feel self-conscious to you, like you are playing yourself in a movie.

It's terrible how quiet it is. Awful. It's making you feel nervous. It makes you wish Yuki or someone else your age still lived next door. Somehow, neighbour-friends are easier for you than actual friends. They are sort of default friends — kind of like Joey, come to think of it — friends you don't have to work at or really participate with short of just simply living in the same building.

Back in the living room, you try to type something, anything, again. You make yourself a deal, your bed calling to you louder than your desire to make this project any good. You will do it without stopping. You bet yourself that you can write it all in not-one-second-more-than-thirty-minutes. You set the timer and type. Force yourself out of you.

At the end of it, the buzzer goes and you stop exactly then, mid-sentence, and hit print. You don't read it over or do another copy. You just staple it together and put it in your bag for tomorrow. Then you lie on your bed and wait for your father to come home. It's late. You can't sleep until he gets home. You know you can't. Until then, you'll read and read and read until you begin to feel squirrelly from all the alternate lives you inhabit. It's only when you hear his keys drop on the hall table and his pocket change hit the jar that you can relax. Until then, you are always slightly tense. Poised for disaster. Brittle. Listening. When he gets home and you hear him coughing or sighing or flushing the toilet, then you are okay.

He comes home after midnight. He was hosting some kind of conference, something that involved dinner, drinks, shmoozing. Probably Cassidy, too. You'll be tired tomorrow, you think, as you snap off the book light and drift into an uneasy sleep, clutching the novel to your chest like it's a teddy bear.

A few days later, your teacher stands at the front of the classroom, holding all of your papers in his hands like they are precious documents that deserve to be under glass. He rubs the top page absent-mindedly. His sweater is the exact colour of newsprint. The sun is sloping through the window, shining in his eyes, and he squints. You can suddenly see how young he is. He hasn't shaved. He looks *almost* cool, *almost* hot. Pretty okay, in fact. How old is he, anyway? He doesn't look *that* much older than you.

Why are you thinking this? You blush furiously, the heat crawling up your neck and making your skin itch as though you have scabies. The teacher is saying that some of the papers were good and some were surprising. He hesitates, then says, Cat. And you can hear, again, the way he feels about Cat, and it makes your stomach cramp up. He asks her to read her paper, which isn't a paper but a poem. You hate her because you wish you'd thought of that.

She reads it perfectly. Her voice dancing, like she's seconds away from bursting out laughing. Like she couldn't care less. Her voice is steady and bored and curls over at the edges with a light kind of sarcasm. Her gaze drifts around the room lazily. You wish *so much* that you could be like that.

The funny thing is that what she reads is totally familiar. Recognizable. Like something you heard a long time ago and are only just remembering. She didn't even write it, you realize. You cough, as though you almost blurt that out but you can't. Of course, you don't say anything. You know *he* thinks she wrote it, he thinks she's brilliant. The tickle in your throat turns into a choking laugh. At him or at her, you aren't sure. Later, you will look up the words you remember and see that the poem was actually written by someone named Merwin. You remember that it won a famous literary prize. Your teacher is much too stupid to know this. But what he does know is that when the winter sun shines low through the window, you can see through Cat's shirt. You can see her breasts. She is thin in a different way than you are. Her thinness has curves. Yours doesn't.

You hate her. You wish she'd be your friend. You want to laugh at her or with her or both. You are overcome by the fact that you are dying to meet her eye so you can say, I know it's not yours. You look at the floor instead.

When Cat has finished reading (it's a very good poem, you have to agree), the teacher says, Ruby?

And you say, Pardon? Which comes out as more of a croak than a word.

And he says, Can you read yours? ... I'm not really asking, I'm telling.

Oh, you say.

Oh, no.

You get up because he told you to, although it's killing you to do it. Is this your reward for writing something he thinks is good? You have to read it out loud? You'd rather jump out of a plane than talk in public. Your knees shake and your hand trembles and you feel like you might cry or throw up or both. But you don't.

It feels like at least ten minutes before you finally drag yourself to the front of the room, and you can see the cloud of boredom and vague disinterest hanging over your classmates. Two people are asleep. Joey is one of them. Probably he's your best friend, although your friendship with him is secret and has lately been limited to when he's drunk and lonely. Everyone except you calls him "Tic." In addition to living in your building, Tic's dad shares an office with your dad. They've been friends forever. You know Joey better than you know anyone, but he'd be surprised to know that. To him, you're like some kind of relative that he horses around with but has never really *seen*. Not really.

You like him. Like, you really like him.

This is something that you hate admitting even to yourself. It makes you crazy to replay in your mind that moment when you thought he was going to kiss you. The snap in his eyes when he told you to leave. You tell yourself that you don't like him at all, that it's just a proximity thing. It's just because he's around. But it isn't. It's something else. Something about the way he smells that makes you blush. You wish you could shut off the crush and have a crush on someone, anyone else. Anyone seems like they would be easier to like than Joey Ticcato, who is really, when you think about it, a complete jerk.

Now, from your position at the little wobbly podium, front and centre, you glare at him and cough hard, but he doesn't move. He's practically snoring. You don't know why the teacher doesn't wake him up. You think, I'll talk quietly, so he won't hear me. Or loudly, so he will.

You think, I've got no reason to be nervous, they won't remember this tomorrow.

You read:

My name is Ruby and I'm the girl that no one notices. You've seen me before, or you've known me since the first grade, or you think my father might be famous, or you remember that I'm the girl from the fire. I am the girl from the fire. I remember it, but it isn't who I am. I'm not afraid of fire, although everyone thinks that I am. I'm not afraid of very much of anything, although I look like someone who would be. I think. I'm sure that's how people see me, because I'm blonde and pale and blush easily.

It's like reading something someone else has written. The words feel strange to you, and slippery, like guppies that have jumped out of the tank and are wriggling around in shag carpeting, impossible to save.

My name is Ruby, and I tell myself that I'm not afraid. I can see things about you that you don't think I see. I know things I shouldn't know. I understand things. I think I'm different. I think everyone thinks they are different from everyone else.

My name is Ruby. Half of what I wrote is a lie, but I won't tell you which half.

At this moment, you pause because you are about to sneeze, but the sneeze doesn't come. You know you must look demented, reading this, which — when you wrote it — seemed vaguely literary and interesting in a dramatic way and now sounds annoying, stupid, crazy and pretentious, as you are all the while trying to either sneeze or not sneeze. You stare at the light for a second and the sneeze backs off. Then you start reading again.

My name is Ruby. I'm a girl who goes to school and does her homework. I don't go to parties. I don't play sports. I'm afraid that one day, I'll be old. I wonder who I will be, in between now and being old. I don't remember who I was before. I hope I know myself when I've moved on. I hope I remember.

I hope no one thinks I'm crazy.

You clear your throat and keep reading, even though at this point you would rather stop than anything in the world. This is torture. This is absurd. This is not happening. Your voice is coming back to you through a long tin tunnel.

I hope I am crazy. I hope people like me. I want to be liked. I want to be taller. I want to be prettier. I want to be more popular.

Here your voice breaks a bit, but you think they aren't listening, anyway. You are very nearly whispering because the tinny-echo sound of yourself is so off-putting.

I want to go to college. I want to know what I want. I want to finish this essay. I want to know who I am. I want to be able to answer that question with something other than my name.

Who Am I? I am Ruby. I'm just a girl. That's all. I have blonde hair and fair skin and I'm not that tall and I had braces when

That's the end. Finishing mid-sentence. You sit down and your face is as red as your name. It's pulsing with humiliation. You are so embarrassed. You want to die, right away. NOW. You want to vanish. You want to kill yourself. Anything, something. How humiliating. Awful. What were you thinking? Why did you write that? Why did you READ it? Which is worse? It's the most embarrassing thing you've ever done. You wish you had refused. You wonder whether you can just drop out. You could just stop coming to school. You're over-reacting. You try to breathe normally. You hate drawing attention to yourself, and blushing and panting is doing nothing to make people look away. You close your eyes. No, that's not working either. Your hand — well, your whole body — is shaking like there is an earthquake of which you are the epicentre.

You look over, quickly, at Joey. You are beyond relieved to see that he is still asleep. His friend Rob ("Robbo," everyone calls him, because no one has a normal name here) bounces an eraser off his ear and he yelps like a poodle. You pretend not to notice. You think you'd like to get up, walk out and never ever ever come back again.

X is staring at you. Oh God. Really staring. He hates you. He is always staring at you, and it makes you feel small and separate. God, you think, that stupid essay. You don't remember writing that or *why* you wrote it. You think, Oh my God, they'll think I'm no fun. Who writes crap like that? It was supposed to be funny or ironic or both.

You hate school. You hate yourself. You can't stop thinking it; it's like a loop in your brain: I hate myself, I hate myself, I hate myself. You look down at the floor until the class ends. They'll forget, you tell yourself. They've already forgotten.

I liked your essay, Cat whispers, smiling at you across the quiet pimply kid who stinks like sour milk and sits between you. She's grinning like you're friends now. You've passed some kind of a test. You aren't friends with her. Your embarrassment is so violent that you almost want to punch her, if only that other kid wasn't in the way.

You nod and say loudly, Yeah, good poem.

You don't have that many friends. You have people who don't frighten you, who you eat lunch with. Cat scares you. You glare at her. You look away. When the bell goes, you grab your stuff and you hurry. You go into the bathroom — the stall at the end with the toilet that never stops running — and wait there until the bell goes again, writing your initials on the wall, over and over again, to the sound of rushing water.

You wipe the wall off with your bare hand before you leave. For the rest of the day, it will look like you've been picking blackberries, the juice smeared across your palm and fingers.

My name is Ruby, you think to yourself. And that's the whole fucking story.

X

4

HERE IS A snapshot of what it's like to be me:

Ka-POW, I say out loud.

I watch the ball explode off the tee and float down the raggedy-ass field so far I can't see it. I need glasses, you know. Maybe you've seen me squinting. But for some stupid reason, I can't seem to bring myself to let anyone know. Honestly, I feel like glasses are for smart kids, book-reading kids, not for me. I can't explain it, but I can't pull off the look, you know? And contacts ... Well, fuck that. I don't want anything *in* my eye. No thanks. Besides, Deer sure as hell can't afford them, and I have better things to spend my money on. I'd really rather not see. What's there to see, anyway? I don't need to see the golf ball once it's left my club. I trust that it's going to go where I want it to go. I know how to place it on the face of my club to make it go anywhere. Why bother checking? I *like* watching the white fluff of the ball floating away from me like the dandelion seeds I blow with Mutt in the summer, lying in the cow field we call a "yard," staring up at the blue cup of sky. I *like* losing the ball into the distance. What difference does it make where it lands? It's not like you can change the path of it once it's started its trajectory. After contact, it's on its own. Doing its own thing.

That's sort of like a metaphor for life, no? I get the feeling that you get what I mean by that. Like it's happening anyway, whether you're looking or not.

I kick another ball from my stash onto the practice mat. I have done this a million times, believe me. Golf is my life. These white balls. This rubber tee. This club.

I line it up. Wiggle the club. My shoulder pinches, so I hold the club behind me and twist and stretch my back and shoulders. It's cold out here today. The air is so hard it's like trying to breathe solid ice. I'm shivering. My skin is prickly from goosebumps, reacting to the air. Should be wearing a parka, but who can practise in something like that? I'd rather be bare-armed, frozen, muscles stiffened up.

Sometimes, I can see how we're all animals, you know? I feel it. Not like animals play golf or anything like that. I'm not saying that. I'm just saying: the way my body moves and twinges and knows things from sense alone. I just like it. Like the way, when I wind up to swing, I can feel my tendons pulling, ligaments retracting. I'm tall and skinny, yeah. But I'm stronger than you think. Stronger than you know. In my head, I'm ripped and fine. Sinewy. Powerful. Different than I look.

You know what else I like?

I like the way people stare at me. I said I didn't, but I do sometimes. I just hate *why* they do it. They do it because they think I'm the next Tiger Woods. If I never hear that name again, it'll be too soon. What's wrong with people, anyway? People have no imagination. Zero. It's like they're just blank idiots waiting for someone on TV to tell them what to think. As soon as Tiger came along, it was like every black kid in North America must be naturally gifted at golf, it's just that none of us knew it until he saved us all. He's like the golfing Jesus of black kids everywhere. Golf is our *saviour*. Or not. It sure isn't going to save *me*. I'm sick of him. Sick, sick, sick. Give me a break. It's GOLF. It's a game, not a cure for cancer. He's just a guy. He's good, but he's not a god.

I'm good. But am I that good? No way. Not a chance.

You know, on some level, he's probably sick of himself, too. It's like somehow his race can't be separated from his skill, you know?

If every golfer on the tour was black, no one would comment. I guess maybe it's like being a white basketball star in the NBA. You just stand out, so people can't stop mentioning it.

Thwack.

Do you play golf? There's a moment when you can feel it, when it's right. The golf club twinges a certain way in your hands. A shudder of vibration. A sound.

I could teach you. Maybe. If you wanted.

Ka-POW.

Yeah. That feels good. I like that.

Deer is obsessed with Mr. Tiger Woods. There's a picture of him on the fridge, smiling, with his huge teeth whitened so much they look like squares of gum. She loves him. Loves, loves, loves him. But not in *that* way. Deer loves Tiger the way other people love, I don't know, the royal family or The Tragically Hip or Jennifer Aniston. The way

Mutty loves Clifford the Big Red Dog. Let's put it this way: we get the freaking Golf channel, even though we can't afford to eat meat more than once a week and sometimes we can't make the rent.

Deer sits in her beanbag chair, stuffing envelopes for extra money, her eyes glued to Tiger's every move across the tiny green patch of the TV.

X, she says. It's your turn next. You could be famous.

Look at that putt, she'll say. That man is not of this world.

Plink, she says, when he gets one in the cup.

I don't hate golf. I don't hate Tiger Woods. I just hate how she loves him.

And honestly, would I want to be Tiger Woods, even if it was possible? For real? I can't imagine myself out there on one golf course after another, week after week. A patch of grass in Scotland or Arizona or Singapore or somewhere. They're all the same, golf courses. The flat greenness of them could make you blind or drive you fucking nuts. I think I'd be like people who get lost in deserts and go crazy from the sameness of it all. Sure, tour players are playing for millions of dollars. Bling bling. That kind of money can buy some kind of happiness. Enough happiness for me. Enough happiness for my kid brother. I have to look out for him, you know. It's not like he has a daddy either.

Ka-POW.

The ball sails off my club like it was meant to be. I shield my eyes from the watery winter sun, which has sunk so low on the horizon it's starting to look lopsided, starring up my eyes with smudges of darkness. Not that it matters. Not like I'm watching the ball's flight. Like I can see that far.

Ka-POW. I slice another one hard into the fence.

I guess one of the big things to me is that golf — it's a *game*. It just doesn't seem worthwhile, you know? Is it enough to make a life? To play a game for money? It doesn't have a point. I want to *do* something, okay? I know that makes me sound like a huge asshole, but I don't care. I want to change things. I just don't know how. Or why. Or if I'll ever really be bothered to do it.

Tiger raises a lot of money for kids, Deer says. He's changed all those lives forever.

I nod. I know it. I'm happy for him.

He also wins. All the time. Every time he plays, he's close, at least.

Me, I've come either first or last in every tournament I've entered. I'm not consistent. Guess why? It's because I don't fucking care. On the range, I'm consistently good. I like the driving range. The rhythm. The mindless repetition.

Blam.

Blam.

Blam.

But on the course? I don't know. I get bored. My mind wanders. Poor Deer. I'm going to break her heart, and what has she done to deserve that?

Ka-pow.

Ka-pow.

I get scared that I'm not good enough.

Ka-pow.

I'm a jerk.

Ka-bang. I swing the club hard and miss the ball by a mile, whacking the ground at least six inches before the tee. The twang goes all the way down my spine and for a second I feel like I'm paralyzed. I hold my breath, count to ten. Like a little kid would. No one is looking at me so no one can see how, for a second, tears sting my eyes. From the jarring of it, that's all.

I can hear my own breath, like it's too loud for the space. I stretch with a club behind my back, pulling my shoulders taut. The pain is there, but it's okay. I can take it. It's not so bad.

I like this empty time. An endless supply of balls. Nothing else in particular I have to be doing. My mind all hollowed out and white and smooth. Hitting dozens and dozens of balls without stopping to think. Well, I do think. You can't stop, can you?

It's quiet, except for the balls being hit. A handful of us in a row, staring down the field. People don't talk. They just do their own thing, everyone swinging and huffing and muttering under their breath. There's a girl — a woman, she's old, probably thirty-five — I see here every Thursday. Fuck, she says. Fuck, fuck, fuck. She always has brightly coloured nails, and lips to match. I like her. She seems tough, but not tough, you know?

Hey, Tiger, my boss says, coming up behind me.

I can smell him before I turn to look at him. Sweat and old whiskey and stale coffee and some kind of cheap tinny-smelling cologne. I finish my swing, the ball sailing clean and pure. It's a darkening blue day, sky open, flat and glassy, like the surface of a frozen lake. Getting colder through and through, ice freckling the grass, air biting my lungs like insects.

Tiger, he says again.

Yeah, I say. What. I hate myself for answering to that. But I told you, I answer to everything. I'm like a dog. You know, how they'll come when you call them, no matter what you say, if you pitch your voice just right.

Nice swing, kid, he says, and claps me on the back. You're getting better. You're gonna be the star of the tour. You gonna remember us when you're rich and famous?

Yeah, I say. Sure thing, Bob.

Bob's a guy who didn't make it. You know the ones I mean. Guys like that'll break your fucking heart. Looking at Bob makes me want to run away. I don't know where. I just want to get into a car and drive and drive. Not that I know how to drive, but I'm sure I could figure it out. (Deer says I can't get my licence until I get a car, and I can't afford a car.) Bob makes me want out of here. Guys like him, they make me furious. The guys who work the golf courses and give advice to the old ladies who clutch their clubs so tightly that their whole bodies careen into the shot, the balls rolling four feet down the slope. The guys with the broken dreams helping the fools who have forgotten what theirs were in the first place.

You teachin' today? he asks.

I shake my head. A couple of times a week, I teach some kids how to swing. Make a little extra money, but not much. I'm not a pro. I'm just an assistant. Nothing people want to pay for, that's for sure. Only the parents who see me and think that, because I'm black, I must be good.

Yeah, well, don't forget to pick up the buckets, says Bob. We don't pay you all this cash to show off, you know.

But then he winks. He thinks he's kidding. I think he's sad. I want to grab him by the shoulders and say, Don't wish this on me. Is this what you want me to be? I don't want to be you, Bob. Not you.

I want to wear suits and be respected. I want to buy Deer a real house that doesn't get walloped with sliced shots every couple of hours. Get Mutt to a real school with other kids so he can figure out how to be one before he drives everyone else crazy. I want to go to Europe. I want to work in a bank or a hospital. I want to wear a lab coat and be interviewed on CNN. Or maybe I want to just get married and have two kids and work at the local car lot. I don't know what I fucking want. How could I know? Seems like choices we make right now are forever. It's too hard to think about it; it's too much.

I concentrate on the shrinking pyramid of balls in front of me.

Ka-pow.

Ka-pow.

Ka-pow.

My nose is running now, dripping steadily. It's raw and sore; I hate that. It's dinnertime and I should go, but Deer will keep it warm, not that that'll make it taste good or anything. She's probably putting it in the toaster oven right now, imagining one of those Golf channel guys interviewing her. Imagining saying, X was always at the range. I always had to keep his dinner warm for him in the oven.

Everyone has dreams. I just wish her dream was about her and not about me.

Ka-pow.

I dream of buying a car that hangs low over the ground so I can prowl the streets like a night cat, all eyes on me. Eyes on my wheels. I dream of moving out of this podunk town and going somewhere where people drink martinis and own sailboats. You know what I mean. A shiny magazine kind of place. A clean place. I dream of all kinds of crap like that. Sometimes I dream about you.

Ka-pow.

That scares you, huh. It sounds creepy, and I don't want you to think I'm creepy, so I'll probably never tell you; I sure won't show you this. This is just rambling.

This is just junk.

Besides, you wouldn't want to be my girl, I know it. I get it. You're just some girl who sits in front of me in English class. Beside me in History. Three rows back in Algebra. At the end of the row in Comp Sci.

Not that I notice.

I'm all run out by Cat, anyway. Emptied, you know what I mean? She's great. You know Cat. She's a lot of person all crumpled up into such a tiny girl. She and you, well, you're different, that's all. Not in a bad way. You would never go out with an asshole like me. You are the smart girl, the girl who's going places. Beautiful, but you don't know it. I can see that in your round shoulders. You can't see yourself. You're too smart to look at me twice, too smart to notice me: six foot three, swaggering down the hall with my friends, all laughing and acting like fucking hyenas. I'm invisible to you, I bet. Like it's snowing and I'm a ghost. I slide past you like ... I don't know. Like a polar bear on an ice cap. You know that polar bears' fur isn't white? It's not. It's transparent. They just blend in to wherever they are, which is almost always snow.

The stupid truth is that I'm only visible to girls like Cat, girls who like to shock their parents by taking black guys home for dinner. That kind of crap still shocks people in this white-bread town. Girls like Cat, who have barbells through their eyebrows, eyes that glitter like knives. Girls who crack their gum like gunshots. Girls with no boundaries and a death wish, who like to climb up high on things and stand too close to the edge and dare other people to tell them to stop.

Not girls like you.

Ruby.

If I was going to describe you, I'd say, Ruby is like an animal in a zoo, I can see her pacing around inside herself. When I see you, I feel dizzy. End over end.

Nah, I wouldn't say that. I don't talk like that, not for real, only in my head. I'd honestly probably just say, Yeah, she's hot. She's okay.

You read an essay in class a while ago, and it choked me up. I wanted to go grab you and carry you out of there. But at the end, you looked like you were going to laugh. Like you were laughing at us. At me. Like we were too stupid to know what you meant when you wrote it. It was a weird freaking essay, sure. I didn't get all of it. But guess what? I don't think you did either. When you were reading it, you sounded surprised, like you didn't remember it said *that*.

When I see you, I want to lie down on the floor in the hallway of the school and let the waxed lino hold me up and keep me from falling through the earth. Have you ever felt like that? Have you?

Crazy. It's crazy.

But if you haven't, you've never lived.

I'm just starting to live now, I think.

Ka-pow.

I know I'm an asshole. I come off like a jerk, I know I do. I somehow can't help it. That's what you're thinking. To be writing this to you and not to Cat, and, well, I don't know. You know how I am with Cat. How I'm using her up. All the while thinking about you with your white blonde hair and brown eyes so dark they look black; they make you look possessed, like aliens on TV with the liquid eyes. There's a word for you: incomprehensible. I'm studying for my SATs. I know my big words. I know *you*, even if you don't know that I do. I know Cat. There's a word for Cat, too. One that won't be on the SATs. It starts with an S and ends with an L-U-T. She can't help it. She needs people to like her; she needs it too much. It's all wrong, but it's true. She throws herself at me so hard it's like she wants to hurt me. It's all physical. It's so physical. That's supposed to be good, right? Everyone's supposed to want that. But the way she does it makes me wonder what happened to her that makes her give herself away so *ferociously*. It's like being attacked. It makes me an even bigger jerk than I seemed before to *say* all that, but I'm honest at least, huh?

Hey, if it makes you feel better, I don't much like myself sometimes either. But that doesn't explain why you don't like me. I've seen your lip curl under, like you can't stand to look at me. Which should make me hate you, but it doesn't.

It makes me want to prove you wrong.

I hope it's not because I'm black. Or because I'm poor. I wouldn't peg you as a bigot, as racist, but I guess you never know. Maybe it's something less than that. Maybe it's easier. Maybe it's just because you think you know something about me.

Maybe you do know something about me. I get the feeling that you do, that you see other stuff about me, stuff beyond the jerky outer parts. I think maybe you can see I'm some kind of hero, somewhere deep down inside. Or that I could be.

Even though I know I'm not. Really. For example, the other night, late, I was walking. Downtown. I don't know why. I guess Mutty had a cold and was coughing and crying and the coughing made him puke, and I just had to get away. Not because I was mad at him, more because I could hear his hurting, and I couldn't help. Deer was getting flustered, rocking him, her hair in disarray; you could just smell the sick-smell of a kid, his face red and blotchy with a fever. You could see Deer's uncertainty, like she was at a loss for what to do, like she'd run out of whatever mum-stuff she needed. I hated it. I couldn't take it. I wanted to get right out of my skin, so I did the next best thing: I walked out the door.

I walked all the way downtown. Went into a 7-Eleven for a Cherry Coke Slurpee. I spilled it on the floor, already a sticky mess, didn't clean it up, but that's not the bad part. The sidewalk was slippery from some new ice, I could see the streetlights reflecting in patches. It was pretty.

Then I heard something. Coming from a parking lot, some kind of screaming.

Bad screaming.

And I should have run over there, found out what was going on. I should have rushed to the rescue. But I didn't.

Some kind of hero I am, huh. I kept walking. I kept drinking my drink, so cold on my teeth it sent a spear of pain through my forehead like a Slurpee lobotomy.

Knife-sharp. The screaming hurt my ears. I don't know what was going on. It was probably just a fight, right? Some pissed off or drunk couple screaming at each other. I checked the paper for the next few days; it wasn't like there was a murder or something, and if there was, what could I have done? Even if I'd run over and looked, even then, what would I do?

Maybe it was just a car stereo too loud. Kids fooling around. A joke. You don't know. I sure don't.

I don't know what I meant when I told you that. I wanted you to see I was more than just a jerk, but then I guess I proved myself wrong. Great.

Still, your own life is probably full of stuff you hate, too. Everyone's is. Secrets that wake you up at night, make you sit straight up and feel like you're choking, and then you remember you're just upset because you're an asshole. That's life, right? That's what people do. You see it all the time on the street. Women biting their lips and glowering at their husbands, fat with rage and pain and unhappy endings. You can see they're with the wrong ones. You can see they've picked the wrong life.

Don't get me wrong. I'm not *settling* with Cat. Cat's great. She's Cat. She's ... well, she's amazing. She's like a string pulled taut on a guitar, all twang and song. I'm seventeen. Fuck "settled." She's my best friend. I like her and I don't like her, but so what? Isn't that what friends are like?

I don't love her, and if she says she loves me, she's lying. To herself. To me. To everyone else. She and I are the same in a lot of ways. We're both running away by staying right here. We both know nothing will ever change except us.

I slice a ball wide and hard and watch it sail toward home. Literally. I imagine it smashing the glass window above the little rust-stained sink. Picture the glass shattering. Why? I'm not even mad. I just think I could do that. That could be a sign, if you're looking for signs, like Deer usually is.

I pack my clubs into the back office and shut off the lights, feeling the darkness draping down into the cold like paint spilling over me. The shadows move. I'm always the last to leave. The last to quit. It's my job, after all. You don't get ten dollars an hour for nothing. I get it for this. Going up and down the rows, picking up the empty baskets, staring out at the darkness, sweeping up the cigarette butts. Throwing empty pop cans into the recycling bin. Straightening the fake grass mats.

All the while thinking, What the fuck am I doing here? Is this what it's about for me?

I don't know what to think. I want to stop thinking. But I can't because when I stop for ten seconds, someone else asks me, "What's next? What are you going to do with your life? What are you going to do? What are you going to DO? What are YOU going to do?" I don't know, I want to scream. I have no fucking clue! Leave me alone. I don't want to make these decisions. College or no college. Cat or no Cat. You, like you're a choice. I know you're not, okay? I'm just saying.

Where to live. Where to go. Choices that do matter, that will make a difference. Deer says I should start applying for golf scholarships at big colleges. Florida. Texas. California. North Carolina. Places with golf teams that have spat out famous guys like Duval and Mickelson and

Davis Love III. I don't belong in a world where people have numbers in their names, you know? As much as Deer thinks that I do. But for a few minutes, I think, Yeah, I could do that. Then I remember that they aren't going to recruit the kid that comes last every other time he plays because he can't really be bothered.

Deer thinks they will. She's kidding herself.

Sometimes I think I'm going to be here in this hole forever. Literally *here*. Collecting the baskets. Shutting off the lights. Cutting across the field to get to Deer's house, where Mutt will climb onto my lap and say, Eggs is home. Eggs is late for dinner.

And Deer will say, That's okay, little Mutty Mutt, we kept it warm for him, didn't we? We kept dinner warm for X.

Eggs, Mutt will say. You want Mack an' Ronny?

He's still stuffed up from that cold, still sounds sniffy, green crust around his nostrils.

Eggs, Deer will say, and she'll pick Mutt up and kiss him like she can't stop, boogers or no boogers, his long blond curls spilling over her face like feathers. Eggs is *always* hungry for macaroni.

Get a haircut, Mutt, I'll say, shovelling the Kraft Dinner into my mouth and tasting nothing. You look like a girl.

I *am* a girl, Mutt will say in his baby voice.

Well, you are pretty, I'll say. Pretty, pretty, pretty ... ugly.

And Deer will say, No, no, never. We'll never cut his beautiful, beautiful hair.

Mutt will giggle — his laugh sounds like a rusty gate — and I'll roll my eyes, and it will be like this forever, like we're an old vinyl record, stuck in a groove in this field and destined to be this way, repeating and repeating and repeating like whacking endless golf balls into the blur.

Ka-pow.

Ka-pow.

Ka-pow.

CA✝

5

CAT SWINGS BACK on the cracked rubber-tire swing so far that her newly partially-shorn hair — shaved and raw in some patches, long and stringy in others — brushes the gravelly, ice-clotted dirt. Meow, she says, her cigarette dropping out of her mouth and nearly landing in her own eye. She laughs.

Careful, says Mira automatically.

Always, says Cat, winking. She twists around to retrieve her cigarette and put it back in her mouth. It feels so familiar there, it's getting so she only feels like herself with a cig. The other day, she noticed that cigarettes and crayons are almost the exact same size and weight. She seriously suspects that this was on purpose, that the crayon companies are in with the smoke companies to make the shape seem like home. She thinks about mentioning this to Mira, but Mira already thinks she's full of conspiracy theories, and she can't stand for Mira to correct her. Not right now.

Mira swings slowly next to her, out of sync. She's still wearing her school uniform: green plaid skirt, white shirt, red tie, with a big yellow parka over the top that makes her look like Big Bird. Mira goes to a different school — one of those decisions their parents made early, that the twins would somehow be better off to have some separation. Well, it worked. Mira has different friends. Different interests. Different tastes. A whole different life. Cat's both jealous and not jealous. She feels sorry for Mira and wishes she could be more like her, and also, she hates her.

So, what's new, she says, straightening up. The chains on the swing are cold against her bare arms.

Aren't you cold? asks Mira.

No, says Cat.

Huh, says Mira. I'm freezing. Where's X?

Working, says Cat. He's always working. He's such a bore.

Oh, says Mira.

Ohh, mimics Cat. She swings for a minute more, the sky tipping crazily around her head. Winds up the chains by spinning, then jerkily unfurls them. How's your sucky school? she asks. You must have something interesting to tell me.

I don't know, says Mira. Nothing special, I guess. I have a debate to do tomorrow that I'm probably going to mess up because I don't even agree with myself, you know?

A debate, mimics Cat. We don't do those at our white trash school. Besides, I'm sure you'll win. Don't you always win?

No, says Mira. I don't.

Yeah, right, says Cat.

They sit together without talking for a while. Swinging back and forth, straight and crooked. Purposely trying to bash into each other without looking like they mean to do it. Mira laughs, a belly laugh. Cat hits her harder. They used to swing here all the time when they were little kids. They used to wear matching outfits, too. They did all that twin stuff. Trading names. Tricking their mother. Well, that's all changed. Now they look different, not in their features but in their mannerisms. Their expressions. Somehow, they took the same basic mould and diverged so much that they barely look alike. Mira's heavier, but somehow, her heaviness is pretty and warm, while Cat's thinness is harsh and brittle. Mira's face is clear and Cat's is spotted with blemishes that she can't stop touching.

Mira's fancy school has a special program for gifted students, which, of course, she is in. She's the twin with the brains. And the looks, thinks Cat bitterly, though she doesn't know why this is true. Somehow, Mira is just better. Slightly smaller nose. A tiny bit bigger eyes. Teeth that are a bit more even. It all adds up to a nicer, bigger picture. Obviously her parents agree, which is why Mira goes to a school with field trips to, like, Paris. At Cat's school, a field trip is more likely to the local jail to watch the prisoners try to act in a play or to somewhere equally crappy and weird.

Cat is the scrap-twin. Like the runt of the litter, even though the "litter" was just the two of them. She got the leftovers that Mira didn't need to be smart and beautiful and everything else.

I'm going to a party this weekend, says Mira. It's supposed to be a big crazy thing. Someone's parents are away. Want to come?

Cat shakes her head. I've got plans, she lies. Mira's parties are horrible for her. Painfully restrained. Boring, quiet groups of people eating pizza and being polite. Cat likes parties where things get broken and people throw up and the police are called to force them to turn down the music. I'm going to hang out with X, she improvises. We're going to do something. Some stuff.

Huh, says Mira. I hope you're careful. When you do *stuff*.

Whatever, says Cat. I'm not stupid.

Are you sure about the party? asks Mira. There's going to be drinking and all that.

Cat looks at her hard. Drinking and all that? she says. You better be careful, sister. You don't want to fall off the straight and narrow.

Mira looks uncomfortable. It's not like I've never had a drink, she says quietly. You don't know.

Yeah, I guess I don't, says Cat. What do I know? I'm sure you get loaded all the time.

Shut up, says Mira.

Who are you going with, anyway? asks Cat. Do you have a boyfriend that I don't know about, too?

No, says Mira.

Mira has never had a boyfriend. Mira's never even kissed a boy, not that Cat knows about, anyway. Mira makes Cat feel old and filthy and used up. Ragged. She spits into the dirt. She's had sex so many times she's lost count. Only with X, but still, it seems shocking to her. Gross. Like it's all blurred together. And, frankly, nothing like she'd imagined it would be like before she'd done it. She'd thought there would be more ... tenderness. Loving. With X, it's more like stuff she's seen on *Animal Planet*:

hump, hump, hump, and just when it starts to hurt more than she cares to take, it stops. And she lets him keep doing that, pretends to like it, doesn't even try to let him know that he's hurting her, that he's maybe, just maybe, not doing it right.

Hump, hump, hump.

It's like he's using her up in some way that she can't pinpoint. Something about how he doesn't really look at her while it's happening, how he's focused on some point in the distance past her head. Something about the fierce concentration on his face. Like he's having to try. Like it's work.

She hates that she's given herself over to this whole thing without bothering to say, "Stop it. This hurts." She hates that it happens so often, the exact same way every time. She hates that she clenches her teeth and gets through it. She hates that she keeps *wanting* it anyway, in spite of how it is. Or maybe because of it. Maybe because it's so untender, so methodical, so hurtful. Maybe that's what feels right.

Well.

Not that she could tell her sister any of *that*. Not ever. Mira is someone who would "make love." Mira would see fireworks: lights and colours. Mira would cry from the joy of it. She'd hear music. Have orgasms. She'd know how to connect. She'd just do it better, do it *right*.

So, Cat starts to say, and then she stops.

The park is empty and the temperature is dropping. Their breath is showing, smokeless clouds hanging in front of them. There used to be a lot of kids in the neighbourhood. There used to be people here all the time, playing baseball or sliding on the swings or walking dogs. Cat doesn't know when that changed. There's a rock in the middle of the park, a huge rock that looks like a small mountain. It has two trees growing out of it and some new graffiti, some kind of spray-painted alien and the initials B.P. and K.B., plus a masturbating stick figure drawn in black felt pen just where the rock face fades to white. The whole rock looks wrong there, like it was dropped from downtown outer space. It's the place, now, where Cat meets her dealer to buy pot. He's just a kid himself, maybe fourteen, probably selling his dad's stuff. Rumour has it that his dad is in some kind of biker gang. Not that Cat cares. He's a nice enough, harmless kid. Just not a park-playing baseball kid like you might expect to find here.

Nothing is like it used to be.

Their house backs onto the park. From here, they can see across the field and into their own kitchen. They can see their parents in the kitchen, talking.

Wonder what they're talking about, says Mira.

Who gives a rat, says Cat.

A rat? echoes Mira.

Rat's ASS, says Cat. Duh.

Yeah, says Mira. I guess.

They both watch as their mother gestures violently with a spoon. When she talks, her Italian roots show. She talks with her hands. She talks constantly and fast. When she's telling a story, she sometimes knocks knick-knacks off shelves with her wild movements.

Probably talking about how great you are, says Cat. Super Mira. What have you done lately?

Shut up, says Mira. Nothing.

You shut up, says Cat. Do-gooder.

Mira laughs, dragging her feet in the gravel.

The sound of Mira's dragging feet or her own boredom or both makes Cat want to scream. She stands up on the baby swing, which bends under her feet, pinching her legs and shoes together. She starts bending her knees and swinging as hard as she can. Twisting. If she swings hard enough, maybe she'll go all the way around. The sky swoops and falls. The air bites into her bare arms. She can feel her body working, like it used to, when she did gymnastics. Gymnastics was different from everything else. Nothing like swimming or lifting weights or any of that. So much more intense and focused. She misses it. Without it, her muscles feel underused, restless. She swings higher. Harder. Mira moves some distance away and watches, hugging herself like she's afraid. She doesn't say anything. She doesn't tell Cat to stop. She never does.

A crow swoops down and lands on the bar above Cat, making a loud caw. Suddenly, weirdly, it comes and flaps so close to her that she can feel feathers on her skin before it flaps off in a black flurry. She pushes herself more, swooping higher than the bird. Higher than anything.

Finally, Cat's legs start to cramp up, so she lets go. Jumps. A second too late. She misses the lowest ebb of the swing and falls farther than she thought she would, lands forward on her hands, knees, belly. It *whoomps* the wind out of her and hurts so much at first, with her palms scraped raw on the ground, the swing hitting the back of her head on its return. She lies low, waits until her chest unsqueezes and grabs a breath. There, there. In, out. Breathe. Mira hovers. Cat gets up. Pushes past her sister and runs loopily over to the monkey bars and climbs up fast. Scrambles, the metal cold and rough on her skin. Then she somersaults over the top bar and drops, eyes closed, just so she can *whoomp* herself again. She lands hard on her heels in the sand. Wobbles backwards, lands on her hands and butt. The sand is cold and damp. Sitting, she sees she has narrowly missed a pile of dog crap. Mira still hasn't said anything. She watches her sister, then she turns around and starts walking slowly back toward the house, head tilted to look up at the sky. She probably has homework to do, thinks Cat. She'll probably *do* it.

Cat has her own homework, but she's not doing it. She has Math questions. She has to write some crappy character thing for English class, which she definitely won't do because of Mr. Beardsley. Asshole. She can flirt an A out of him without even trying. She bites her lip when she talks to him, and looks down. She squirms in her seat and watches him turn beet red.

She could fuck him, she thinks. That would get her an A, for sure. But she doesn't want to. She loathes him, really, and loathes the way he always looks at her like she *would* if he wanted her to. She'd rather prove him wrong than follow through, although maybe it would be better. Maybe it would be different. Maybe it would be worth it.

I am a slut, she says out loud. Fuck.

She has to study a chapter in her Science book about the disgusting insides of a frog. She has a test on it tomorrow. She hates the dissecting, the organs, the formaldehyde smell. Hates the dead frogs splayed out on their black tar beds, white labels on pins like flags marking their insides. She heaves a sigh that hangs in front of her like a mini-thunderhead. Really, she can only get away with not doing the English. She'll *have* to do the others. She's not getting good grades, so it really doesn't matter, but she should probably try to suck it up. Only half a year left, after all.

She jogs in place on the grass. Does a cartwheel. Mira hesitates, looking back at her. Starts walking toward her, then changes her mind and turns for home. She calls something, it might be, It's too cold! Or, You're a toad!

Cat pulls her cell phone from her pocket and flips it open, but it's off. Probably broken from the fall. She whacks it against the slide, and the lights flash on then off again.

Fuck, she says out loud.

She wonders whether X has called yet. He usually calls when he gets home from work. She's thinking maybe she'll break up with him when he calls. If he calls. She's getting that vibe again, like he's losing interest. Like he looks through her when she talks, and it's making her antsy.

Besides, he's just not as much fun as he looks. He's beautiful, so what? He's getting boring. She wishes he would surprise her and do something unexpected. Get a tattoo. Steal a car. Rough her up. Anything. She's hungry for him to change. She climbs up the slide, but she can't slide down. Her legs are too warm on the cold metal slide, and she sticks there at the top.

Sometimes she feels so trapped here — on the slide, in the park, in her life, in suburbia — that she just wants to *go*. Get on a bus and disappear. Wants to move to New York or L.A. and become a famous actress or a singer or both or anything. Anything but this. She hates the suburbs, the identical white houses. She hates Mira's neat sweater and coat from The Gap and the way that Mira keeps circling back, waiting for Cat to get moving, to get off the slide, to come home.

She walks down the slide, the metal collapsing slightly under her feet, sounding like cymbals. Does a round-off, onto grass so cold it crunches under her sore hands. Takes a deep breath.

Argh, she screams.

Mira stands and waits, head cocked like a puppy's.

Cat sits in the grass for a second. Lights a cigarette with a match struck on the sole of her shoe. She's dizzy, inhales big, blows rings to bug Mira.

I'm going, shouts Mira. It's too cold for this.

Cat ignores her. She takes a pin out of her shirt pocket and sticks it fast and hard it into the fleshy part of her palm. Pulls it out and lets it fall in the grass. The exit always hurts more than the entry. Then she gets up and runs to catch up to her twin.

Hey, don't *wait* or anything, she says, grabbing Mira's hand with her bloody one before she gets to the gate so they can go into the house together.

You must be so stupidly cold, says Mira. I don't know why you can't wear a coat like a normal person. Your hands are frozen.

I'm not cold, Cat lies.

Liar, says Mira. Why do you have to lie about it? You're obviously cold.

Whatever, says Cat. I'm not cold.

That's totally fucking annoying, says Mira.

What did you say? asks Cat, clutching her head with her free hand in fake shock. Did you say "fucking"? Oh, my head.

Cat, says Mira, trying to shake her hand free. Could you just ...?

What? says Cat.

Nothing, says Mira. Forget it.

Don't fight, girls, says their mother, leaning out of the kitchen into the front hall. Her face is damp and sweaty from cooking dinner, hair stuck to rivulets on her overly made-up forehead. Dinner smells great, even Cat has to admit that.

What's for dinner? she asks. She lets go of Mira, whose hand she was holding so tightly she's left marks, she now notices. She touches her mum on the shoulder, surprised as always at how soft her mother's flesh is. Sinky, like quicksand. Smells good, Ma.

Sometimes she doesn't actually think she wants to leave, now or ever. She could live here forever, eating her mum's stews and pastas and casseroles and bread. Never alone. Never hungry. Never not looked after. Mira is going to Stanford next year, but Cat hasn't heard anything in response to her early admittance applications. Not that this is surprising at all — early admittance is for A students, overachievers, geeks, brainiacs, Mira. She knows she isn't going to Stanford anyway, early, late or probably ever. She'll stay in this lame-ass town, go to a community college, become a dental hygienist or something equally awful. She shudders.

No, no, no, never, she swears, not that. She runs her hands — riddled with tiny cuts from the park's gravel — under the hot tap until they sting and scald. Then she makes her way into the dining room and sits at the doily-encrusted already-laid table and waits for her sister and her parents to come and join her.

Ruby

6

EVEN THOUGH IT'S sort of your own private joke with yourself, sometimes you think you really *are* going crazy, like this is what crazy is. Feeling stuck in your own head. At odds with everything and everyone and mostly with yourself. That, the idea that you aren't crazy is itself a crazy idea. Do crazy people know that they are crazy?

You kind of want to ask your dad but you won't. He's been extra-jovial lately, like he's getting confused between his TV book-promoting persona and his real self. His joviality makes him unapproachable and almost creepy. It's like Santa has been let loose in the mall on the off season or something. He's started making up nicknames for you that push you back. Yesterday he called you "Sugarplum," and you almost threw up, a reaction that makes you think that the crazy idea is not crazy at all. Crazy people probably throw up a lot. In the middle of conversations. When they are given dumb nicknames.

Probably the very fact that you can't stop contemplating your own craziness means you are crazy.

You should be crazy.

People think so. Especially people who have read your dad's book, you're starting to sense. You really should read it. Why can't you read it? You should force yourself to read it.

But you can't.

Anyway, whatever it says must somehow imply that you are a fun kind of crazy, a zany kind, a Cat kind, an understandable kind. An approachable kind. People are approaching you.

You don't like being approached. It makes you uncomfortable. They can go ahead and approach your dad; he asked for it. But you didn't ask for it. And you don't want it.

Which in itself is probably also crazy.

People would accept (even seem to want) a kind of dollar-store insanity from you, like, insanity-lite. They would understand it — admire it, even — and you could take Zoloft or Prozac or lithium or all of them or none of them. Maybe you could have electroshock therapy like in that Winona Ryder film. But no, that's too extreme. Too ugly and creepy and weird.

When you saw that movie, it reminded you a bit of the boarding school books you read when you were little. It made craziness look not that bad. It actually looked kind of fun, living in a dorm with a bunch of other people who accept all your weirdnesses because you've all already been written off by everyone else. Zap, zap, zap. You could make your brain flatter and easier, and you'd maybe be happier or less confused. But then you wouldn't be yourself.

Besides, the joke is that you aren't unhappy. You're just lonely, even though you are always around people. The *approaching* people. People like the bullied kids at school, like you can somehow help them. People like the aunties, who swirl around constantly, like a flock of annoying mosquitoes, just waiting to get close enough for their brush with fame. People like Courtney and Joanne, who probably only so forcibly hang out with you because you are as close as anyone in this school has come to being famous. Not the people you want to be around. The people you would never approach.

You shake off your thoughts without moving, although you imagine them scattering away from you like droplets of water off a wet dog's fur. Where are you? Oh, right. Here. You are *here* at a pricey restaurant with your father and his newest girlfriend, the much-mentioned Cassidy. It's all hushed thick carpets and dark wood furniture and multiple glasses at each place setting.

You don't usually think of the women who cling to your dad's sweatered arm as "girlfriends" because they are usually so ... adult. Women friends. But this one is different. She *giggles*. You sort of want to punch her. Pull her hair and run away.

What kind of name is *Cassidy*? you want to ask. It sounds like something you would call a golden retriever.

But you don't.

So, *Cassidy*, you say in an effort to sound interested. What do you do?

I'm a doctor, she says. Specializing in gynecology.

You nearly choke on an ice cube. Which probably would have been okay because she could have saved you, performed an emergency tracheotomy, using a Bic pen and a steak knife. Or at least the Heimlich, squeezing the ice cube out of your airway professionally, without breaking any ribs. For a second, you can practically see it happening, the ice cube popping out of your mouth with all the force of your lungs and shooting across the room into someone's fancy cold soup two tables over.

A doctor, you repeat. Well. You must be very *smart*.

Just goes to show that you don't actually have any sense about people after all. You would have pegged her as a model, like, not a real model but one who works at car shows or poses in calendars wearing next to nothing. Or a stewardess, the sort who doesn't care whether you call her a "flight attendant" or an "air hostess," who wears her skirts just a bit too short and her makeup a bit too loud. Your father stares at her while he eats, sort of gawps at her really, like he's never seen such magnificent chewing before in his whole life.

Oh, God, you think, please don't be in love with her. No, you say out loud.

Yes, says Cassidy. I'm a doctor. I suppose I am even what you might call "smart." Does that surprise you? She smiles widely, like someone about to devour the head of a doll, showing off her perfectly capped, white, even teeth.

No, no, no, you say. No. You can't think of anything else. No.

Your dad shoots you a look that says, Watch it, kiddo. Or Sugarplum.

Cassidy wears her immaculate overly highlighted hair in a French braid. You haven't worn your hair like that since you were nine and used to figure skate. You quit when you were ten. You were tired of being bruised and cold, blue-lipped and tired. You were tired of the fact that your father's girlfriends clapped for you in the stands, even when you fell. You hated the way they braided your hair and took pictures of you like you were their own kid. You were tired of the fact that your father was usually too busy to come.

You cross your eyes at him, but he isn't looking. You have a funny, almost overwhelming urge to pour your water over her head, just to see what she'd do. Can almost see it beading off her shiny, shellacked hair. You have to remind yourself that you're sixteen, not ten. Instead, you push your cuticles back with one of the three knives in front of you, not caring that it's really a pretty gross thing to do in public. Cassidy watches with disdain or disgust, not even bothering to pretend you don't repulse her, much like the look she probably gives to giant tumours that she carves out of people on a daily basis.

You wish your mother wasn't dead, wish it so hard you can practically see her shimmering to life next to you. But if she were alive, would she still be with Dad? You hate yourself for asking this, even in your own head, but ... really. Well, your mother didn't look anything like this woman. She wasn't in this league, this buffed, polished, rebuilt, perfect league.

A waiter discreetly pours you more water, gives you a clean knife. You nod at him. Say, Thank you.

You wish you had a normal family who ate their meals at home and did normal things. You abhor restaurants.

You sigh.

How was school? your dad asks.

Fine, you say. Just fine.

Do you have a boyfriend? Cassidy asks. You can see a certain cruelty in her face. Maybe it's her high cheekbones. Or her contact lenses.

Sure, you say. Lots.

No, she doesn't, says your father. He laughs, a short explosion of sound that turns into a sneeze.

How would you know? you mumble into your glass.

What? he says.

Nothing, you say.

You hate yourself for feeling belligerent and childish. You wish the food would come out of the kitchen. You wish you could really make wishes and have them come true. You'd wish for something amazing. Something unimaginable. You'd wish to go back in time and undo the fire, which was your fault, though no one ever says it. You know it's true. Although you don't remember that part very well.

Or at all.

Maybe you just dreamed that part, but somehow, you think it was real. Your fault. Was it a candle? The moving white curtains catching and slowly flaring up. Or was that a movie that you saw? In your nightmares, that part is almost pretty, like a flower blooming into full life. Still, you wake up screaming. All the time. Over and over. The paralyzed kind of sleep scream that feels like it's coming through layers of wool clamped over your nose and mouth, the muffled fear that makes you feel you're being suffocated.

Your father says you can't possibly remember the fire, but maybe that's just what he *wants*. He wants you to forget. He wants it to be tidy and quirky and funny and easily analyzed and fixed and cured and sold on national TV. He *should* know the truth: that you can remember and that you wish you couldn't. He should know how to fix *that*. He's the shrink, after all, impossible to forget now. Someone from another table has recognized him and is pointing from behind a menu. You wave sarcastically, the woman blushes and lowers her eyes.

You point to your father and mouth, It's HIM!

The famous, funny shrink.

The woman won't meet your eyes. You should really read that book, you think. See what he's said about you.

No, no, no. You aren't ready. You might never be ready to see yourself through his eyes.

One thing he says TO you is that children don't remember stuff, that they can't. But you do. You remember falling. You remember flames. You remember your mother's voice screaming, Ruby, Ruby, Ruby.

You remember tasting grass and dirt, landing hard, the breath being smacked out of you in a *whoomp* that felt like dying. Gasping. Your father picking you up. The way he held you so hard you almost threw up or stopped breathing again.

You've constructed a memory based on stories you've heard, he says. That's what happens.

And you want to believe him, you pretend you believe him, you tell yourself you believe him because it sounds plausible, after all. He knows these things. What do you know? You're sixteen years old. Sixteen doesn't know anything. You know enough to know this.

Cassidy clears her throat again, it's like a nervous tic, or else maybe she's choking on a hairball. What's your favourite subject at school? she asks.

Fuck you, you want to say.

I don't know, you say. English, I guess.

English!

Yes, English.

Oh, says Cassidy. I always liked Science the best. And Math. And Gym. I was a cheerleader. God, I loved school. Loved it, she repeats with new emphasis. Just *loved* it.

Of course, you did, you say.

Ruby, says your father. It sounds like a warning.

You sigh again. There isn't enough air in this place. It's making you light-headed, all the sighing. Hyperventilating probably. Again. Because you're thinking about it now, you can't stop. You sigh once more, as deeply as you can.

You try to think of things you can say about school, but nothing comes to mind. School makes you anxious. You hate school. School gives you a place to go, to be. You love school. You wish you fit in there like everyone else. You wish you had friends other than Joey, who ignores you, anyway. You almost feel like telling Cassidy the truth. You don't have a favourite subject. Sometimes you don't go to class. You just sit outside instead, waiting. Like you're waiting for a bus, only you're not. When you are inside, you keep your eyes down on the waxed red linoleum floor and breathe into your sleeve, which smells like perfume. Why is the floor red? you wonder.

To hide the blood, people say, like that's funny.

Blood — the idea of it, the sight of it, even saying or thinking the word — usually makes you faint. The real colours that spill out from people's insides, those send you straight to nothingness. The first time it happened, you were only six. You were riding bikes with Yuki, the girl next door. Eating an ice cream sandwich with one hand, pedalling madly, barefoot. It was summer and the ground was hot, you could feel the terrible heat rising up from the asphalt. You were squinting into the sun when you heard her shriek. Her foot in the bike chain, the blood spurting out, her ice cream sandwich melting on the pavement. You hit the ground hard, unconscious. You checked out.

Fade to black, you always think before you faint, which is often enough that it's become a bit of a joke between you and your father.

Daddy, you say when you feel it coming on, I'm going to faint.

Fade to black, he says, and catches you. He always catches you.

Thinking about fainting makes you feel faint. You stare up at the lights, crystal chandeliers woven with what look like dead twigs. Focus.

You see the colour green above your father's head, a smoky green, grey at the edges. The colour of worry. You can't stop him from worrying. You don't want to know that he's worried. It's not your job, he has said, to worry about me. I'm the parent. I take care of you, not the other way around.

But you want to take care of him. His sad eyes watching you eat your cereal in the morning. The notes he leaves on the table saying where he is, when he'll be back, the dumb jokes he tacks on the end as if by adding something that's supposed to be funny, he'll prove that you are both cheerful people. The way he knows when not to talk to you. You wonder whether he's like an animal, whether he can smell your fear.

Cassidy swings her long, blonde braid over her shoulder and starts talking in a low voice to your father about a patient. You feel yourself drifting, bored, concocting fantasies about nothing. Behind Cassidy, there is a wall of mirrored glass. You look in the mirror, and you are just you, Ruby Ruby Ruby. Hair so blonde it's nearly invisible, not rich and golden like Cassidy's, pulled back from your face so tight your black eyes look like eight balls staring out. You actually look like a ghost of yourself in contrast to her sparkling, solid, shiny-lipped, white-toothed presence. Sometimes you wonder vaguely whether maybe you did die in the fire and that this, what you see, is just a ghost. Does a ghost know it's a ghost? How would you know?

But then you spill your water, pour it over the edge of the table, onto your lap, and it's cold and you know that you're alive. Of course, it's only there for a split second before a waiter swoops in to take care of it. Your pants he can't fix, though, wet and clammy on your skin. You wouldn't feel cold if you were a ghost. You wouldn't feel so empty, so hungry.

How long does it take to make a burger? you interrupt.

Patience is a virtue, your dad says. Oh, virtuous girl.

Whatever, you say, and you roll your eyes. You see Cassidy shooting your father a sympathetic look. You want to take a mouthful of water and aim it at her, shoot from between your teeth, her fake big smile dissolving in a jet of cold, like the Wicked Witch of the West melting in *The Wizard of Oz*.

The waiter plonks your burger down in front of you, taking away the four forks you won't need. You're so hungry you don't even bother to listen to your dad and Cassidy and their dumb chit-chat. You stuff the burger into your mouth as though you haven't eaten for months, meat burning juicily on your tongue, raw onions stinging your winter-dry lips.

The truth is, you haven't eaten all day. Sometimes, you forget. Sometimes, you don't want to. Sometimes, you go as long as you can without food just to see how long you can last. It's not because you think you're fat, it's just because you're interested. You want to know what you can survive.

You have been afraid for a long time. You are afraid of the following things: death, your father leaving or dying or both, failure, spiders and throwing up. You are afraid that suddenly you might forget how to talk or how to breathe, and when you think this, you immediately hyperventilate. You are afraid that you are invisible, that no one sees you, that you are here just to see them, to observe.

You like observing.

You chew, you swallow, you observe.

Stare.

Watch.

Remember.

Hours later, when you finally get home, you type it all up on the laptop your dad gave you for Christmas, the laptop that you wanted, only better. The best of the best. Only the best for you, he says. For my angel. You stay up late that night, tap-tapping on the keyboard in your room, writing it all down, and for what? For whom? You rewrite it until you like the way it flows.

Why?

It doesn't matter why, you tell yourself. You just do it. Perched up high on the twelfth story of the building where you live with your father, with city lights visible from your open window, you type yourself.

Like this:

Wednesday. Today was a good day until dinner. It was cold but not snowing, although the air was jagged, as though snow is coming. At lunch, Courtney and Joanne asked me to sit with them, so I did. We (or they) talked about a party they went to last weekend. Apparently Robbo threw up in someone's washing machine. "Hilarious!" they said, but they laughed like they were nervous about it. About him. They'd invited me, I just didn't want to go. Parties scare me. Honestly? I'd rather stay home and read. Embarrassing if anyone found out what I read. Last weekend, I read *Alice in Wonderland* for the fourteenth time. I don't even like it anymore. I don't know why I keep re-reading it. What am I looking for in there? It reminds me of a riddle, so I guess I think it has an answer, but probably it's just a weird story. It reads like someone else's hallucination. I read somewhere that the author was into little girls. Sick. Don't know if it's true or not, but I hope it's not. If it's true, it ruins everything. It makes it all wrong.

C. and J. talked about going to a peace rally this weekend but I don't think they know what they are fighting for; I think they just like the crowds and music. I feel so separate from them. Half the time, I have no idea what they mean when they say "you know?" I say "sure." But I mean "no."

They talked about getting their tongues pierced. Everyone's doing it, or so they said. I didn't faint, but I almost did. Grey spidery feeling of fading. I pretended to be looking at something on my shoe, but really I was putting my head down. Remembering to breathe slowly.

I got 100 percent on my Chemistry test, and I felt stupid for it. Does that make sense? Getting a perfect score makes you stand out. I could feel the other kids looking at me and hating me, fleetingly. Just a flash of blue loathing. You'd think hate would be red, but it isn't. It's blue and muddy. Love is red. Happiness is a pale orange that looks like smoked salmon. I caught X staring at me in English. I turned around and he was staring right at me. His eyes are so blue, I'd never really noticed. Big pupils, black like stones. He scared me. There wasn't even a colour around him. It was like there was a complete void surrounding him. There is something about him. I don't know what it is. He smiled at me and said something. I think he said "Ruby." But maybe not. Why would he say my name? I smiled at him. It felt like a lot.

After school, I went out back and watched while Joey smoked a joint in the janitor's shed. He had his well-worn copy of *Alice*. He thinks he's going to make it into a series of poems or songs. Probably songs, he figures.

I love *Alice*, too.

That's what we have in common. It's a weird thing, huh? It gives us something to talk about, too. I think it makes me seem okay to him because I get it, his weird love for a little girl's book. He quotes it sometimes. I think he's memorized it, but he got embarrassed when I asked if he could do it off by heart. The whole thing.

I bet he could.

He did "Jabberwocky." He does that to make me laugh. Or maybe he doesn't mean to make me laugh, maybe I'm just laughing. He makes me nervous.

While we were out there today, he put his hand on my knee, then, like he noticed that he had done it, he jerked his hand away like it was on fire and said, "Sorry." He wasn't drunk.

I am the kind of person that people apologize for touching.

Had dinner with my father's new girlfriend. I guess I'm too old to call them Auntie now, thank GOD. She's a doctor. She says I should call her "Cassidy." She bites her nails. I hate her and I hate her hair. Dinner was a burger. It was awful. I threw it up as soon as I got home. Dad probably thinks I'm bulimic, but the truth is that his stupid girlfriend makes me nauseated. They're in the living room, talking. If she's here when I wake up tomorrow, I'm going to ... I don't know. I won't do anything. I hope she's not. I don't want her to be. I don't like her. I wish ... never mind.

Your own diary irritates you. Your own thoughts. So you stop. You close the lid of the laptop and stare out at the city. It's a quiet place. There is traffic, but just a low hum. Your apartment building is near the water, and a siren sounds when the bridge goes up and down to allow freighters and other large vessels to pass underneath. Next door there is a vacant lot that is usually full of garbage and shrubs and birds and drug dealers or people who look like drug dealers. When you walk by, you see used needles and it scares you. Sometimes you hear drums coming from that lot. Sometimes people scream. But not seriously, just loudly. There is a nightclub close by. People spill out, drunk people. They stumble into the vacant lot, probably to pee, and all that emptiness makes them yell. Fuck you, they'll scream suddenly right under your window and you'll run to the window and look down but they'll be gone already. You like the drums. You think that there are some people living under the bridge. First Nations people, you think, but you don't know. They beat drums late at night and chant. You hope they are chanting something spiritual, but when you listen closely you almost think you hear them saying, Fuck you and fuck you and fuck you, too.

When you fall asleep, you dream that everything is new. You dream that you are pretty and that there is applause and laughter when you speak lines that must be memorized but that feel true. You dream your mother isn't dead, but then in your dream, her hair whooshes up suddenly in a fast flame like fireworks, and she smiles and starts to melt. When she melts, you cry, not just because you're sad but because there is something terrifying and repulsive about the melting flesh. You wake up feeling sad and exhausted. You go into the kitchen for a glass of water and you pass your father's open bedroom door. You can see him in there, the lump of his body under the sheets. He's alone. You can smell his stale sleep smell.

This is a relief.

X

7

X, SAYS CAT.

Come on. I want to talk.

Yeah, I say, rolling over on my side and opening one eye. The carpet on Cat's bedroom floor — what you can see of it between piles of discarded clothing and garbage — is this dog-sick yellow colour. No one looks good against vomit tones. No one. Cat looks all messed up. What, I ask, reaching over and squishing down her hair, which is sticking up a hundred different ways, making her look like a skater boy and not like my girlfriend. Not like anyone's girlfriend. I hate myself for thinking it, but she looks ugly. For a second I want to push her away, then I don't. I'm too tired for one thing. I close my eyes.

Hey, she says. Don't sleep.

I'm not, I say.

X, she says. I've been thinking. You know? And here's the thing. The thing is that I want to see other people. You know.

No, I don't know, I want to say. But I don't. I close my eyes and open them again. Like that could change something.

What? I say.

You know *what*, she says. You heard me.

No, I don't fucking know, I say into the floor. What comes out is not words, but a sound in my throat that feels like I'm choking. I can smell the carpet. It smells like plastic or rubber, or maybe that's me. Condom-scented and sweaty.

Who are you going to *see*? I say, hating myself for sounding like I care. I sound like an old man or like a kid about to burst into tears. I don't care, I tell myself. I don't need her. I don't need anyone. I don't even like her. I sit up. The carpet is scratching my skin and I have to get out of here. I feel like I can't find any air.

I'm not breaking up with you, asshole, she says, twiddling her barbell. I'm just saying I think we should both, like, you know. Hook up with other people if we want. You should. Maybe you want to.

No, I don't know, I say. I don't know. Who? I don't want to. Why do you think *I* want to?

And this is bad, but I'm thinking, *Ruby*.

You don't love me, anyway, she says. So who gives a fuck? I don't know what *I* want, why should you?

We're in high school, I say. No one loves anyone.

X, she says, staring at me hard with her blue eyes staring right through me, not blinking. X, she says, people love people, you fucking moron. Just because you don't love me don't mean *shit*.

Doesn't, I say automatically before I can stop myself.

Holy crap, she says. Sometimes you are such an extreme *jerk*.

Then she laughs. She sits up and laughs. Laughs so hard she starts to sweat, or maybe she's crying. Her face is wet, anyway. She reaches across me for a handful of cold fries and starts eating them one by one. Staring at me.

I have to go, I say. I pull my pants on without bothering with underwear. Without bothering with anything. I have to go to work, I say.

We're not broken up, she yells after me. She's still laughing and eating. I start to laugh, too, not because it's funny. It isn't funny. But because I can see her there lying on her yellow carpet laughing and laughing and you can't not laugh to see that. She has a laugh that cracks you wide open. Her laugh makes her beautiful. She laughs like she's hurting you.

When we first hooked up, we were fifteen. I didn't really ask her out. Not really. I just stumbled into her at a party — drinking more than I ever have since — and she kissed me. Well, sort of. She locked on and I fell into her. We've been together ever since. She is the first girl I ever did it with. We did it at Robbo's house. His parents were away somewhere, they're away all the time, though who would leave a kid like Robbo alone I don't know. He's in trouble a lot, taking crazy risks, doing stuff I couldn't imagine doing. He'll try anything. Drugs. Skydiving. Diving with sharks. Whatever, seriously. Anything.

He had parties all the time, every weekend it seemed like, so often they lost their edge. Anyway, Cat and I did it in Robbo's parents' bed. Dumb thing is that it didn't feel like I thought it would, like I'd pictured it. I mean, mechanically I guess it did, but not inside. It made me dizzy. I mean, obviously I *liked* it. It's sex. It's just *likeable*. I'd be an asshole if I said I didn't like it, and I'd be lying. I can't explain it, it just wasn't what I was expecting. Wasn't as otherworldly. Wasn't as emotional. Wasn't as *connected*. In a way, I sort of blamed her for that. Like if it had been with someone else, it would have been different. But there's something about Cat. Even when you're doing it with her, she's still holding you at arm's length. I can't explain it.

Cat cried. I remember that. Actually, I think she threw up. She was drunk. We both were. Romantic, huh?

Sometimes my life is too hard for me to take.

As I'm leaving Cat's house, I bump into her sister Mira in the hall. She smells like outside, like snow flaking in wet air. Mira is nothing like Cat. She's got great posture, for one thing. She carries herself separately from everyone else, like a model or someone who is already famous. She's carrying a knapsack that looks like it has about forty-six books crammed into it. She smiles at me, but her smile says "I don't care about you" or maybe even "I don't like you." She has a crust of mucous or something dried under her nose but even that doesn't make her look bad, if that makes sense. Just makes her seem more human.

Hey, she says. She has the same voice as Cat. Sometimes it freaks me out. Same voice, same eyes, same nose, same mouth, same everything more or less, completely different person.

Huh, I say. I never know what to say to her. I don't want to talk to her.

Okay, I say, I gotta go.

Are you okay? she asks. But I pretend I don't hear her.

I run away, slow at first and then faster and faster. I'm kind of laughing, but I'm not really. Maybe I'm crying. I don't even care, I think. I'm not even sad. I think of you, and if you broke up with me, I think I would cry, and somehow, the thought of it does make me cry, but nobody can tell because I'm running and sweating. I'm running so fast my tears can't catch up.

I'm a bad runner. I run looking crazy. I do. I don't look good like some people do when they run. Those African guys who run barefoot in the Olympics, running like fucking antelope across the savanna. I wish I ran like that, but I don't. I run toes out, knees grinding. I run like an ostrich with its feet stuck in the mud. I look like an idiot. But I don't care. It feels like flying. It does.

I should know.

I run faster and faster, jumping over ditches, dodging parked cars. In my head, I'm running like a movie star. I pat my pocket for my imaginary gun. I imagine shouting, Cover me, I'm going in. Bang, bang, bang.

It's about two miles from Cat's house to mine, over lawns, through a gravel path in the woods. I run the whole way, winter-taut wind screaming in and out of my lungs, and I think that there was a guy who did a three-minute mile, right? Where is that guy now? Takes me so much longer than that, I feel embarrassed. I'm the shame of my fucking race, I'm sure. The only black guy in North America who can't shoot hoops to save his life and who runs like a girl.

The pavement turning to gravel, turning back to pavement under my feet, and the houses passing crookedly behind me, and my heavy knapsack banging me in the ass with every step — I don't mind it. I don't know what I'm feeling. There are crows on the power lines, staring at me. Black beady eyes. I caw at them as I thunder past, arms flapping. Crows creep me out, all that staring, all that blackness.

How was your day, honey? Deer asks, as I collapse over the doorstep and onto the floor. My chest is heaving.

Same old, I tell her between breaths. Nothing new.

You working tonight? she asks, standing over me, her long blonde braid swinging back and forth like a rope. Smiling. Nudging me with her foot.

Is it Tuesday? I ask.

Yup, she says.

Then I am, I tell her. Every Tuesday, the same. Every Tuesday, every Wednesday, every Saturday.

She should know that by now, but she doesn't remember. Deer just floats along from day to day. I don't know how she does it. I'm scared I'm going to be like her. Vague. Somehow emptied out. I don't want to be like that. It pisses me off in a way that makes me want to put my fist through the flimsy wallboard, makes me want to *react*.

Fuck, I say, and hoist myself up and push by her into the bathroom. Ignoring her. Ignoring Mutt, who pulls at my pants and says, Eggs, you stink. Woof.

I know I stink. I don't need Mutt to tell me that.

Woof yourself, I say, growling ferociously.

He steps back. Falls, really, *bumpf* onto the floor. He's so small, though, he doesn't have far to fall. He's not hurt or anything.

Woof, woof, woof, he says, and scrambles to hide behind the couch.

In the tiny bathroom, I sit down on the toilet, which is purple. Who has a purple toilet? It's like whoever designed this piece of junk trailer went really far out of their way to make it the ugliest thing in all of creation. I reach over from where I'm sitting and turn on the shower and let it blast for a while before I get in, let the room steam up so the steam fills my head and I can stop thinking about anything.

I get in and wash away Cat. Scrub myself hard. Did she break up with me? I don't even know. I can't even tell. I really am stupid, I think, swishing some soap around in my mouth and spitting. I'm stupid. No wonder you won't look at me twice. No wonder you see right through me. And then I think, why am I thinking about you when I should be thinking about Cat?

I'm sick in the head, I am.

I'm an asshole.

Hey, I'm just saying what you would be thinking if I gave this to you, that's all. I'm just being honest with myself. Or you. Both of us.

I get out of the shower and towel myself off, hang the towel around my waist, head back toward my bedroom. Mutt is playing on the floor, building a castle out of blocks. Same blocks I played with when I was a baby. You can see tooth marks on them from where I used to bite them when *I* used to pretend to be a dog. He's just like me, only a different colour.

Mutty, Mutt, I say.

I stack the blue on the red and make an arch out of the smaller yellow ones. He kicks it over and grins at me.

Hey, I say.

Yeah, he says, real cool for a three-year-old.

Never get a girlfriend, I tell him.

Okay, he says. Okay, Eggs.

Okay, Eggs, I repeat. Don't forget it, kiddo.

Don't say stuff like that, says Deer. He'll remember that. Don't mess with his beautiful little head.

Huh, I say, and I go in and get changed for work.

Peas out, says Mutt.

He thinks that's hysterical. I tell him it's supposed to be "peace" but he can't say that. I worry about him. Worry that he'll never learn to talk. Worry that he and Deer will live forever in this trailer, braiding each other's hair. He's three years old, for fuck's sake. Almost four. Peas out. What a kid.

The range is busy Tuesday nights: two-for-one buckets, baby. Can't beat a deal like that. Golf is a rich guy's sport, but the rich guys like a deal even more than anyone else. Even in the winter, people come out, hitting bucket after bucket of balls to nowhere. I earn my ten dollars an hour driving the cart back and forth, scooping up the balls. People always try to hit the cart, and the snap of the ball on the wire cage that protects me gives me a fucking heart attack every time. I wear headphones, listen to my music, but I can't avoid the strikes. It's like a video game, and I'm the target. Everyone does it: old ladies, young kids, everyone in between. Even the pros do it, to show off for their students.

As soon as I get going and thinking about something, BAM, someone hits me again. Jerks. They might as well make it like pinball and have this cart light up and flash when they hit it. 500 points! Ding! Ding! Ding! I can just imagine these business guys going home after hitting a bucket. Going home to their wives and saying, "I hit the cart today, 200 yards, yup." The funny thing is at least half of them are probably lying. When they hit me, I was probably only seventy-five yards out. They're just practising their short game.

I drive back and forth really slowly, trying not to think, because, if I do, I'll think about Cat and I don't want to. I force myself to unfocus, let stupid stuff drift into my head. School stuff. Robbo and Tic cut out all afternoon today, leaving me alone, bored and sleepy.

You weren't there either. Where were you?

I screwed up in Home Ec, which we have to take. I don't know why. Last term, we sewed these stupid-looking bags. I gave mine to Deer and she uses it as a purse. Still. That must be love, huh. It's seriously the ugliest thing I've ever seen. Today, I had to cook a stupid chocolate pudding on my own, without them. Which meant I had to cook *and* clean up. I burned the pudding and my hand. Stupid bastards. Sometimes I hate them, but they're good buddies, you know? They're my people.

Cat's wrong, I think. I know about love.

I love all kinds of people. I've known Robbo and Tic since we were five years old and all went to the same daycare after kindergarten. We've all been best friends ever since. People think it's funny because I'm so tall and, let's face it, dark. And they're not. It's like when a cat hangs out with dogs or something. People stare when we're together. It's not my fault that they grew up to be the smallest, whitest guys in school. They aren't related, but they look like brothers. Cigarettes hanging off their lips all the time. Almost everyone I know smokes. I don't get it. Do they know nothing? Haven't they ever watched those ads on TV? That one where they squish the dead guy's artery and all that crap comes out would be enough to make me quit if

I'd ever started. All my fucking friends will be dead from lung cancer before we're even thirty at the rate they're going. Robbo and Tic, man. They're something else. They look like they were born with cigarettes.

The girls would like them if they weren't so short, Cat told me once. They're badasses. They're hot.

I think she even said she'd *do* them. Sick thing is that she probably would. If they were taller.

At the time, I was pissed. But now? I don't care. Maybe I don't love Cat, or maybe I do.

The thing is, I *know* her. She pretends to be a lot harder than she really is. It's all a game. She isn't knife-sharp and dangerous at all. It's a stupid act. I think it's because she's jealous of Mira. And Mira's probably jealous of her. One thing that I'm noticing lately is that no one seems happy. Especially not you, but that's another thing altogether, isn't it? You aren't Cat.

You're you.

I can't think about you all the time. It's bad. I know it. It's *obsessive*. If anyone knew how much space you took up in my head, they'd think I was a stalker. The truth is I'm just scared that I'm just an idiot, probably like my own dad.

Why would you ever even want to talk to me? Why would you bother?

Bam, another ball ricochets off the cart. If not for the wire, it would have taken out my right eye, crushed right into the socket.

Just once, I'd like to stand out here at the 150-yard flag and start hitting the balls *back* with the Big Bertha driver that Deer gave me on my last birthday. It's an ace club, man. It's the best. I don't know how she could afford it, but I love that club. I imagine getting out of the cart in slow motion and lining up the shot. And then I picture myself just pounding buckets of balls back into the row of players. Ping, ping, ping.

Bam.

I turn the cart around and hit the gas. Head back up toward the ball room to empty my load into the machine that spits them all back into the old guy's buckets so they can hit them out there all over again for me to pick up. It's starting to get dark and the lights are on. I love the way the course smells after it's rained, that wet green grassiness of it. I'm just slowing down to pull into the little bay where I park to off-load the balls when I look up and I see you.

You.

What are you doing here?

I almost say it out loud.

What *are* you doing here? Can't see why you'd be at Mac's Discount Golf and Range at 6:30 on a Tuesday, but you are. You're laughing. I hardly ever see you laugh. I can see your teeth glinting in the lights that have come on over the stalls. You have really nice teeth. Small, white and even. This is going to sound stupid, but in some ways, you remind me of a rabbit. I'll never show you this. You'll never read that. Now I know for sure. As soon as you start describing the girl you like as a rabbit, you know that what you're writing isn't really for her. It's for me.

I guess it always was.

You're laughing up at some guy. Some guy I can't see properly who is putting your ball on your tee for you. An older guy. I hope it's your father. If it's not, I'd be pretty surprised.

I'm looking so hard at you that I drive right into the concrete divider. I swear, I give myself whiplash. I'm such an *asshole*. I can't believe that happened. Of course, there's a huge crashing sound and the balls all spill out of the back. I look like a complete idiot and I think, well, that's okay, you can always kill yourself because really it doesn't get much worse than this.

But it does, get worse.

Of course.

Because there is Bob yelling at me, Tiger, Tiger, are you all right, kid? Are you okay?

And everyone's crowding around, and I've got the smallest cut in the world over my right eye and it trickles. A little rivulet of blood. People are panicking and Bob yells, He's bleeding!

I'm about to say, No, I'm not, I'm fine, when I look up and there you are and I swear, I pass out. I'm not kidding.

Stars. Blackness. Nothing.

And then Bob's there with a cloth, pressing it on my head. A cold cloth, which is actually a golf towel that smells like old shoes and cow manure.

Bob, I say, pushing him away. You'll get me all infected. What's wrong with you?

I'm so embarrassed that I'm shaking like a girl. God, I say in my head, if you exist get me out of this. Now. I'm not kidding.

That's the closest thing to a prayer that you'll ever hear from me. I'm freezing. I can feel my heart beating hard and out of control. Shit, shit, shit, I think.

I stand up and my legs feel wobbly, but I swagger anyway. I can't help it. You were here. I look around, and you're gone. Of course, you're gone. But it doesn't matter,

I know I'm grinning. I feel good just from having seen you. That's so stupid. I can't believe this. I can't believe how you make me feel.

You must have a concussion, Smiley, says Bob. You're acting crazy. But if you're so fine, get out there and move that cart.

So I do.

I'm walking home when it happens. I warn you now, this is where the story gets weird. It does.

It's dark. There aren't any lighted streets running between the range and the trailer. Just the fields, a long, winding gravel driveway and the cows. A few ugly old barns, half-fallen down. I don't know why they're still standing. In the dark, they look haunted. They look like something from one of those stupid horror movies where teenagers are constantly getting killed in their underwear by crazy homicidal maniacs with a hate-on for youths.

The moon is pretty small, a sliver with a halo around it from the cold. It's not exactly lighting my way. I've got a headache throbbing deep in my brain, a slow, pounding pain. But, weirdly, I feel really good. The headache reminds me of the crash. And that reminds me of you.

Ruby, I say out loud. It seems creepy to say your name.

You make me talk to myself. I'm probably crazy, do you care? I think crazy people are probably generally happier than the sane ones. I'd rather be crazy, if this is what it feels like. I feel light. I feel golden.

I feel like a jerk for thinking things like "I feel light. I feel golden."

I sing your name. Ruby. I don't know any songs about

Rubys but I'm sure there is one. I think maybe I'll look some up on the internet when I get home. Oh, yeah, we have a computer and all that shit because Deer makes money doing billing for a bunch of doctors who are too afraid of technology to get their own computers. They drop it off on Friday afternoons. I always think it looks like they're making a drug drop. These guys (okay, and the occasional woman) are wearing their silk ties and driving their nice BMWs and Mercedes and Hondas, dropping envelopes off at the trailer and trying not to step on cow crap on their way to the drop box outside the front door. You can tell it's beneath them. Deer says they're mostly scared of computers. I think that's funny. Yeah. Like they can cut you open and take out parts of you and put you back together again, but they can't figure out how to press the "on" button on a PC.

I'll google the name "Ruby." I'll make you a CD of Ruby songs. Yeah. I like that. It's romantic, like a mix tape. Of course, I can't give it to you. Smile and say, Hey, I saw you at the range, here's a CD I made for you. Sure. That could happen. Not. You'd see right through me. You'd see what I wanted, even though I don't know myself.

I just want you to see me.

Maybe I do have a head injury. You're like a song that's stuck in my fucking head. I can't stop. I can't get you out.

I should make a CD for Cat, I decide. Not that she'd want me to.

I can see the lights of the trailer in the distance. I'm about a thousand yards away when I sort of stumble. I don't even know what happened. Maybe I tripped on something, but I look down and I don't see anything. It's like the world just tipped a bit and I didn't tip with it. I fall forward and try to catch myself, and then the most fucking bizarre thing of all time happens. I'm not making this up. It sounds crazy to me, too, so don't sweat it.

Ready?

It's like suddenly I have wings on my shoulders. You know that feeling when you take a big feather and wave it up and down and you can feel the *whoomp* as it pushes against the air, the pressure that birds must feel when they fly? I felt that.

Whoomp.

And then I was up. Not just up, but UP. I felt it in my shoulders. It was like I was a goddamn bird or something. I realize there is no way of saying that so it sounds like anything other than the effect of a massive head injury. Hey, maybe I had a brain hemorrhage and didn't know it. I'm not saying that's not as much a possibility as any other thing. All I know is that I was falling, and then I was up so far above the trailer that it looked like a tinker toy.

Then I got scared. I'm afraid of heights. Very afraid. That's ironic, huh? First kid who can really fly, and he's afraid of heights. So I came down. Somehow I knew how, like the wings that I couldn't see were guiding me. Sounds fucking ridiculous, don't I know it. But I know what I felt. That was it.

What would you have done?

As I glided down, night air leaking off my wings like water off a paddle, I just knew how. I knew how to glide. I knew how to land. Which doesn't change the fact that I missed the spot I was aiming for, and when I landed, I did fall. Hard. On my knees. Like a baby bird can pretty much fly right away, but you see them falling off the wires when they're learning how to land.

Of course, I fell right in a stinking heap of cow dung. But who cares? My heart was beating loudly, like a thousand drums, I can tell you that. I thought it was going to explode out of my chest. I thought I could taste blood.

My body felt so unbelievably weird. No kidding. But weird in a familiar way, like it feels when you run a few miles or like it did when Cat made me go bungee jumping. A rush.

I feel wild.

I feel alive.

I stand outside for a long time trying to get my head together. I feel like I've been shattered, dropped from a big height on a concrete floor. I feel like I've been glued back together the wrong way, only the wrong way is better than the right way. I am better than I was before.

The first thing I think is that I have to tell you. But then I remember that we don't know each other. Not really. You recognize me because I'm the black kid. I'm Tiger freaking Woods. I don't know you.

I kneel down on my badly bruised kneecaps. The ground is dry and cold and harder than slate. I stay down for a while. Just kneeling there. Then I take a breath. And then another. I feel like I'm gasping for air. It stinks, sure. But what can you do? It's a cow field, for God's sake. I'm so used to it I barely even smell it any more. When you grow up in a field of cow shit, you stop noticing. Believe me.

Hallefuckinlujah, I say out loud. Once my heart seems to normalize, I stretch my arms out in front of me. They look normal. A bit blurry, but I told you, I know I need glasses. I try to feel around to my back to see what's sprouted there. I half-expect to feel feathers, but I just feel my damp T-shirt that's stuck to me with sweat.

I don't even know what to do. I feel like whatever's just happened has made me too big to fit in our little trailer. Like I'm so enormous that if I go in there, I'll fill up the whole space. I'll squash Deer and Mutt. I won't be able to breathe.

Has anything ever happened to you that's so weird you feel locked in place, like you don't know if you're coming or going? That's how I feel. I stand there until Deer pokes her head out the door and says, Phone is for you, X.

She looks at me funny. I wonder what she saw. How long she knew I was out there for, just kneeling in the field like a great fucking moron.

I go inside and pick up the receiver. For a second, I think it might be you. I don't know why. Well, the day couldn't get much stranger, could it? Why shouldn't it be you?

Yeah, I say, my voice cracking.

X?

Yeah?

It's me, says Cat.

Yeah, I say. I can still feel my heart beating. Not so crazy now, but erratic. Like there are two pulses in place of one. I can hardly hear her. It's like my ears themselves are beating. My whole body is beating.

I'm sorry about before, she says. I was freaking out.

Yeah, I say. I'll talk to you later.

I hang up. The thing with Cat is that when I talk to her, I feel empty and heavy at the same time. My heart thud thud thuds in my skull.

You okay, baby? asks Deer.

I have a headache, I say. Which isn't even true any more. That stopped the minute I took off, the minute I took *flight*.

Head dick, says Mutt.

Yeah, I say, I'm the head dick around here, you got it?

Got it, he says, stabbing a Brussels sprout with his fork. Dick.

I sit down and eat and none of us say anything, which is weird because it's usually just chitter-chatter so much you can hardly stand it here. It's like they knew that something had changed. Something no one could talk about. For a second, as I'm chewing a hunk of ham, which sticks between my teeth and tastes like tin, I think about blurting it out. Saying, Hey, I just flew way up into the sky. I want to tell them what it felt like. But I don't do it. I don't know if I could even explain it. Or describe it.

I chew and swallow.

Chew and swallow.

But inside, I'm exploding. It's like I can feel all the blood cells ricocheting around in my veins, and I can feel my heart squeezing. My hand shakes. I'm overflowing. I'm full of an energy I can't control. I try to keep my eyes on the plate, on the bright pink ham, on the pattern of faded flowers on the edge of the mustard dish. I try to see the potatoes. I can sure taste them. Salty, buttery, sweet. Everything seems sharper, brighter, clearer than before. It's crazy. I wonder if this is what it feels like to go insane.

I cough. Just because. I almost need to make sure I'm still in control. You know? I cough again. And then Mutt coughs because he's a copycat. I look up at him and he looks back at me, and in his big huge eyes I think I see something. I think he can tell.

Eggs, he says.

Yeah, I say. What. I open my mouth wide and show him my chewed up ham.

He creaks with laughter.

What was I thinking he was going to say? Some secret of the universe? Something wise?

How was golf today? asks Deer.

Oh, I say, closing my mouth. Uh, it was good. I hit my head.

What? she says. How?

I tell her that I lost control of the cart, and I show her the lump so small you can't even tell it's there. I tell her that I'm fine, that it's nothing, but I'm not really fucking sure that it's true. Is it true? Am I fine?

She gets up and looks so closely at my head that I can see the pores on her nose, smell her breath. For some reason, it makes me want to hug her. Tight. Like the way she hugs Mutt. Instead, I duck my head out of her reach.

I'm fine, I tell her. Really. Forget it. I put my glass of milk down so hard it spills.

Oops, says Mutt.

X, says Deer. Come on.

For a second, she looks kind of scared. Do I scare her? I'm her *kid*. Sometimes I feel like the only adult in the room. When her big wide eyes are looking at me like that. Like a kid's. It makes me mad. It makes me feel like I don't belong. Then I remember how it felt to be *up* there. How small this trailer looked from the sky. How everything flowed out beneath me like a painting. It makes this whole thing — the trailer, dinner, Deer, Mutt — everything, everyone, seem surreal.

Um, um, um, um, says Mutt.

The end, I say. Good story, Mutt.

But um, um, um, he says. Um, the end.

It's not the end, I say. I got homework. This day won't ever end, huh?

Uh huh, he says.

Uh uh, I say.

Are you okay? Deer asks again.

Yes, I snap.

I stomp into my room, shaking our whole home. I want to go to sleep. I want it so *bad*. I want to check out for a while so I can think. I want to figure this out.

I can't sleep. Ridiculous. My heart is racing.

I sit up on my bunk for a long time. I feel like I can't breathe properly; the air is too thick. I'm dizzy, but I'm not. I stare outside through the dirty glass and think, what the fuck? What does it mean? Does it *mean* anything?

I'm scared.

I prop the lamp onto my shoulder and try to do my homework, but I can't concentrate. Close my eyes, but I know sleep is a million miles away.

Flip through the homework again; none of it makes sense. I'll get it off Robbo in the morning, I figure. He'll let me copy, on the off chance that he's done it. He always copies mine; it's about time he paid me back. Fuck homework. It doesn't matter. This just doesn't matter.

I'm sweating. I can't take it. The tinny air, the sound of Mutt and Deer giggling in the other room. The home-work that looks like Russian or something. If this doesn't matter, then what does? I feel like screaming.

After what feels like hours, Deer tucks Mutt into his bed, pats me on the arm. I flinch. Her touching me feels like too much. I listen to the sound of her brushing her teeth, getting ready for bed. Soon it's so quiet I can hear the numbers on the clock flipping over. It's one of those pre-digital clocks, with numbers that actually turn over. From the seventies. I count to sixty between each one. I count my heart beats. I count Mutt's breaths. I'm wide awake. I strip down to my T-shirt and boxers, realizing I'm still fully clothed. Now, sleep.

But sleep won't come. I wait and wait.

I think hours go by. It feels like it.

The rooms are so close together I can hear Deer sighing and turning. I hear the slithery sound of her bedspread sliding off her and her legs kicking the sheets. She doesn't exactly snore, but she makes a weird smacking sound with her mouth when she's dreaming. It's driving me fucking nuts. Like a dripping tap. My head kind of hurts, but not a lot.

There's no air in here. It's like sleeping in a submarine. The air is cold, but thick. Soupy. It smells of burnt dust from the electric heater.

I push the blankets back as quietly as I can. Swing down off the bunk, jam my pajama pants on. Creep outside without shoes. I don't want to open the shoe cupboard because it squeaks. I don't want to wake up Mutt or Deer. I check the clock, and it's almost four in the morning. It's a bad time to be awake. Surreal. It feels vaguely imaginary, like I'm not quite in myself.

I go out through the half-screen door and jump down the three steps. I stand in front of the trailer in a small pool of light from the solar lights that illuminate the front porch. I don't know why I stand in the light. It's not like I'm afraid of the dark or anything. I feel stupid just standing there, so I stretch as far as I can. It feels good. It's cold.

There's my breath in front of me like it always is at this time of year, hanging there like it's waiting for something. There's the gooseflesh on my arms and legs. There's the ache of being too cold. I breathe deeply. I try to feel grounded. I don't have anything on my feet, so my feet are bone-chilled. And then I realize why I came out. Why I've been so anxious and restless and uneasy.

The thing is that I have to try again. To see if this is real or if it's just something I made up, a hallucination or whatever the hell it might be.

I do it. I just think about it for a second, not even that long. I can feel my wings stretching. Unfolding. Like they were there the whole time. Taking off feels like you're releasing a breath that you've been holding. It does. It's like that, times a thousand. Times a million.

I stay pretty close to the ground. I don't really trust myself not to fall. It's so fucking amazing, and I can't believe it's me. I wish I could describe better what it feels like. It feels exactly how you think it would feel. It feels natural.

I fly around for a while. Not far. Over the driving range. High enough that I can't see the flags clearly but low enough that I'm not clearing any treetops or anything. I feel so quiet inside. I can't explain it. It's like I'm liquid. I don't know. It's fucked up, okay? I never said this was easy. It's not easy to understand. Not for me, anyway.

I stay out for some time. I don't know how long. I go all around the neighbourhood, listening to the sound of myself moving through the night. The slow flapping of wings. Everyone's lights are out. They must be sleeping. Everyone's dreaming. I think of all the dreams everyone is having right now. All that craziness. I think of all the people who can't sleep, who are lying there counting the hours. All the people who are having nightmares they can't get out of. I feel really peaceful. I don't do anything. I just fly for a while and then I stop on the roof of a building, estimating the landing just right, falling onto my toes first and then heels, rocking back a bit but not falling. I look around, wish I had a cigarette even though I don't smoke. It just seems like sitting here smoking would be some reason for stopping. Maybe next time I'll bring a snack. It sounds crazy, I know. But I want some Doritos. A hot dog. Something.

Maybe this is happening for a reason. Like Batman. Maybe I should search the city for signs of crime and do something about it this time. Do anything. But I don't even see any cars moving. Nothing is happening here. Besides, just because I can fly doesn't mean I'd be able to save anyone from anything. I could fly down and scare the shit out of them, but what good would that do?

I wait until the sun starts to rise and then I go to the edge of the building. I sit there with my legs dangling off the edge. I feel like a jumper. If anyone sees me, they'll probably think I'm suicidal. Maybe they'll talk me down. Suddenly, I'm really goddamned embarrassed to be up here in bare feet and my pajamas, which are too short in the leg. What if someone sees me?

I'm feeling crazy, feeling out of control and yet calm. I go to the edge, which is about fifteen storeys up, and I just let go — keeping my eyes wide open — and fall for a few seconds. I'm feeling so afraid I'm going to fucking throw up, I'm going to die, I'm going to faint, and then I just spread my wings.

You'd think that after that night I'd have, like, a trans-forming magical day. But I don't. It sucks.

Completely.

For one thing, in the morning it's freezing cold and rainy. It keeps almost snowing and then changing its mind. Frozen rain is the worst. It's like being pelted with bullets. Ice bullets. I'm soaked by the time I get to class; my cold pants chafe and I'm really fucking irritated. The one thing I'm looking forward to is seeing you, but you aren't there.

Hey, I say to Tic. Where's Ruby?

Why? he asks, squinting at me suspiciously.

No reason, I say.

She must be sick or something, he shrugs. How should I know?

I don't know, I say. Forget it.

I wish I hadn't asked. Last thing I need is for him to start some stupid fifth-grade rumour that I have a crush on you or something. I'd never live that down.

Forgotten, says Tic, banging his head against his desk.

He does shit like that. That's why we call him "Tic." Well, partly because of his last name, but partly because ever since we were kids he's been a bit ... off. He bangs his head. He shouts weird shit in the hallway. He's not a bad guy, he's just a little messed in the brain.

What up, bro? says Robbo, slumping into his desk next to me. His hair is soaking wet and dripping into his eyes, which he doesn't bother to wipe. Cheeks red like he's been skating.

Nothing, I say. I'm so distracted that I forget to ask him for his homework. We just sit there, waiting for the bell to go. Waiting for something to happen.

Why do you suddenly care about Ruby? Tic asks again, loud enough that a few people hear.

I don't, I say angrily.

So, why'd you ask? he insists.

Fuck off, I say, cuffing him in the side of the head just as the teacher walks in, slamming his books down on his desk.

Hand in your homework, he says.

And that's when I remember that I didn't do my homework and had no time to rip off Robbo's. Shit, I think, staring up at the ceiling.

Xenos? says Mr. Unhappy-in-His-Work. Where is it at, my man?

I hate it when teachers talk like that. What IS that? Some kind of groovy seventies lingo?

I shrug. Forgot, I say, like I don't care.

He doesn't say anything. Doesn't yell. Just raises his eyebrows at me and writes something down in his book. It can't be good.

What happened to your head? he asks, eyeing my bruise.

Nothing, I say.

The day gets worse from there: I flunk the English test because I forgot to get the answers from Tic, who got them from his brother, who took this same class two years ago. Same tests. We memorize the answers; it's easier than learning anything. Anyway, I didn't forget, I just didn't feel like talking to him. I thought he might want to talk about you, and I already felt like I'd given myself away. I used last week's answers, which I still remember: BCAAACBAAD. Fat lot of good that does. I'm such a moron.

Cat has lunch with me. Or at least she sits next to me drinking a Coke and glowering. She isn't talking. She looks mad and sad.

What's up? I say.

Nothing, she says. Same old shit, different day.

Yeah, I say.

Mira's got a boyfriend, she says.

Really? I say.

I guess, she says. He's a shithead football player.

Huh, I say.

I guess you don't care, she says. Forget it.

I care, I say.

But the truth is that I don't.

Cat glowers at me. I try putting my arm around her, but she shrugs me off.

I gotta go smoke, she says.

Fuck. I can see that she's mad. But I don't get it and can't be bothered to ask. What the hell have I done wrong? Nothing, that's what. The girl all but breaks up with me and now I'm in trouble? What's up with that? I let her go. And just sit there, staring off into space. Ignoring everyone. There are hundreds of people in the cafeteria, but I feel like I'm all alone. You ever feel that way?

Finally, I get up and run through the blood-red hallways to the front door. I step outside. It's fucking freezing. There is nothing worse than being wet and cold. I hate it, but I don't care. For a second, I think about flying off, but people would see me. For some reason, that's more than I can handle. I just walk. Nowhere. Around the school and back. By the time I get in again, I'm late for my afternoon class, soaked and with chapped, numb hands and wishing I was anywhere but here.

By the end of the day, I'm in a bad-ass mood, so when Cat, Robbo and Tic come up and say, Hey, X, come with us, we've got something to do, I go.

CA✝

8

CA+ SI+S IN the car and roars the gas impatiently, snapping her Juicy Fruit gum. The boys are taking forever, and she wants to get going. She's revved up like she gets when she's going to do something crazy. Something wild. Yeah, she knows it has something to do with Mira and her new perfect football-playing boyfriend. A white guy, natch. And the way her mum goes on about him and how great he is. Nathan-this and Nathan-that. They met him for all of five minutes and they've known X forever. Two years. Bigots. She hates them. Nathan is half-Italian. Great. X can't compete with that.

She pushes the car's cigarette lighter in and tucks a cigarette behind her ear so she'll be ready when it pops. Her new haircut is slightly itchy. The shaved patches were supposed to look like something, but they didn't really work. What was supposed to be one kind of pattern looks more like, if she's being honest, a disease. She touches the bare skin of her scalp where it's coming through. She kind of likes the way it feels. Soft and bristly. It doesn't look right, but who cares? The rest of it is long enough and messy enough that it doesn't matter. She runs her fingers through it and shakes it into place. Sings to herself. Turns the stereo up loud enough to make the car shimmy and shake. The school parking lot is full of students, milling around. Waiting. She moves the car from one spot to another just to watch some cheerleading girls jump out of the way. The bus stop is right in front of her, crowded with the losers who don't have cars.

She catches Ruby's eye and drops her gaze. Ruby freaks her out, with her big dark staring eyes. When Ruby looks at her, it makes her feel uneasy. Like the other girl is reading her thoughts, or worse.

She half-smiles, half-sneers. Testing the water.

Ruby doesn't smile back. She probably can't even see her, the windows steaming up from the heater and her wet clothes. The music crackles in the speakers and Cat turns it down slightly so they don't blow. Cranks the heat up further. In spite of the hot air blasting from the vents, Cat is always cold. She's been cold her whole life.

Finally, the boys tumble into the car. Tic and Robbo in the back, X in the front looking apprehensive. Cat wishes he wasn't such a granny.

Granny, she says. How's it going?

Did you call me Granny? X says, looking annoyed.

No, she says.

Tic and Robbo laugh. Punch each other. Light up a joint.

Not here, idiots, she says, revving the engine again. The little car's wheels spin against the gravel. She half-thinks that X is with her and that Robbo and Tic are friends with her because she has a car. Her parents gave it to her on her sixteenth birthday. And it's not an old car, either. It's brand new. Embarrassing. She wanted to paint it up right away. Paint a mural on the side or a bowl of rotting fruit on the hood. Something unexpected, quirky, edgy. Beat it with a chain. Take the suburban newness off it and turn it into something she could imagine driving. It's hard to be cool and edgy when you drive a Honda Civic, even one with zebra seat covers, a back seat full of fast food wrappers and a trunk full of beer-bottles.

X wiggles the heat knob.

It's already on, she says.

Yeah, he says. It's hot. I was turning it down.

Leave it, she says. It's my car.

Fine, he says, opening his window a crack. He leans his head back on the seat. She looks at him out of the corner of her eye. He looks tired. He's so good-looking she feels like something in her chest is shattering like glass blown too thin. She's loved him forever. Really loved him. That's the whole problem, she knows it. He doesn't know it, doesn't know about the love, doesn't know she feels that way. He thinks she's just a good-time girl. Well, maybe she is. She's no Mira with a Harvard-bound boyfriend and ... and what? Really good posture.

She sings along a bit to the music while Tic and Robbo horse around and X ignores her. In a way, she feels more at home with them than she does with her own family. They're like a dysfunctional family of sorts, she thinks. She and X are like the parents, sort of. And the other two are definitely the kids.

Pipe down back there, she says, glowering at them in the mirror.

Where are we going, anyway? X says, not opening his eyes.

Nowhere, she says. Somewhere fun.

She lights another cigarette and blows the smoke out in rings. X coughs and glares. He hates smoke. She blows the rest out in a sharp, pencil-thin stream in his direction. She knows he's worried about the whole breakup situation. She wants him to be worried, to fucking *care*. Secretly, she wants him to ask her to stay. To never leave him. She could imagine her life just fine with him or without him. She could carry his bags on the tour. Hang with the other players' Barbie-doll wives. Or caddy for him. Newscasters would talk about how they were high school sweethearts. How she was always there for him.

Or not. She could move to New York. Become a photographer. Be so hip people would be both in love with her and afraid of her.

She has a feeling that the second scenario is more likely to unfold in her future. Not the admiration and fear, but the *leaving*. She's not going to be anyone's wife. Who is she kidding? No one would choose her. Not when there are girls like Mira around. People marry Miras. They don't marry Cats.

Not that she fucking wants to get married or anything. She snorts.

Are we there yet? Robbo whines from the back seat.

Yeah, echoes Tic. How much farther?

Not much farther, she says, in her most maternal voice.

I'll never be a mother, she thinks. She's only sixteen. It's just that the minute she met Mira's Nathan, she got an unsettling premonition of Mira's wedding, Mira's whole life. Handsome husband, university degrees, great job, perfect kids. And she couldn't help seeing hers, too. And it wasn't as pretty. Bad boyfriends, dropping out of college, some kind of drug culture that keeps her scared. Maybe she'll end up working in a skanky hair salon, waxing people's bikini lines for minimum wage. Or worse, a chat line. She could be a telephone psychic. No matter what she pictures, it doesn't look very glamorous. Or fun.

She guns the engine, and the car skids on the slippery road.

Jesus, says X. Be careful. He cringes as though that would protect him if they were in an accident. She does it again just to make him mad.

Hey, he says. Don't. He reaches over and steadies the wheel.

Don't take care of me, she says between clenched teeth. I know how to drive. More than I can say about you.

Don't be a bitch, he says.

Fuck you, she says.

Mummy and Daddy are fighting, says Robbo in the back seat.

No, Mummy, squeals Tic.

Oh, shut up, you two, says X. Or you'll be grounded.

They pull into a gravel driveway a few minutes later. The darkness is filled with heavy fir trees, branches bent low under the weight of the frozen rain. The building looks like some kind of warehouse, abandoned, dark and depressing.

Where *are* we? asks X.

Surprise, Cat says, getting out of the car. They all follow. Robbo slips on the icy pavement, curses, dropping a case of beer. Lies on his back until Tic and X pick him up. Patches of puddles turned to mini ice rinks crackle underfoot. At the entrance, Cat produces keys on a Grover keychain from her pocket and opens a huge door, some kind of shipping entrance. Throws a light switch.

Holy shit, says Tic.

Oh, MAN, says Robbo. This *rules*.

X just stares. Cat tosses back her head and laughs in a way that she imagines is breezy. To try to get him in the mood.

I'm making a bit of money cleaning up this place for Uncle Troy, she says, looking around. It's closed for the winter.

She admires the place. She is making money but not much, and she isn't doing much cleaning. Mostly she smokes dope in the turret while the workmen do their thing, then idly sweeps up afterward. What she's earned, she's already spent on clothes and cigarettes. Uncle Troy thinks she's saving for college or some crap like that, but then again, he doesn't know her very well at all. Never bothers to really ask. Assumes she's Mira, that they're the same. Gets them mixed up.

She grits her teeth and glowers at her surroundings. Scaled-down plastic buildings made to look like a messed-up fairy-tale town and an overly fancy castle, all held together with colourful slides and tunnels and, the highlight, a net-encased bridge hanging between the town and castle, fifty feet up in the air. Impossible to fall from, but still dizzyingly high.

In the summertime, Troy's Toy Town is full of screaming toddlers and other assorted brats. Now closed, it smells stale. Empty. Hollow. Scented with dusty plastic and Lysol.

Sure, it's made for little kids. Really little. Like four or five. Built for birthday parties. But Cat knows they'll be able to have some fun here, too. Sure they will. A couple of beers and a spliff and it'll be more fun than any of them have had for *weeks*. Impulsively, she reaches over and kisses X, a big smack that feels foreign and comical and just wrong. She realizes that she never kisses him. Well, maybe while they're having sex. He never kisses her. Ever.

He pulls away from her, kind of pushes her back. She shudders.

Let's party, she says, swinging away from him, fast, fast, fast. Like a monkey, up onto the castle's kid-friendly rope ladder with a bottle of beer hanging from her teeth.

Tic and Robbo are right there with her at first, then they go in the other direction. Crawl into the tunnels. Their voices echo off the insides of tubular slides. There's shouting when one of them lands in a pit of plastic balls. X wanders away, not playing. Not sliding. Cat can see his silhouette climbing up a safety staircase on the outside of one of the toy structures.

X is *sulky*, she says to the others.

Baby, they yell.

Ouch! Fuck you!

No, fuck YOU.

There are the sounds of a mock fight. Then silence. From somewhere, one of them turns on a sound system, and radio noise blasts out through the speakers in a rush of static thunder that immediately blows one speaker with a gunshot bang. The fuzzy music sounds crooked, coming from only one side, but still, it makes Cat feel crazy and brave. Or maybe that's the beer. She doesn't care. She feels good. To tell the truth, she doesn't feel good that often. She hooks her legs through the rope ladder, dangles upside down. Throws her empty beer bottle past the safety net and toward the concrete ground, where it splinters like light.

Don't DO that, X yells. He's leaning on a plastic turret, perched there like he's about to fall or jump about ten feet up. The crash pads that normally line the floor are stacked up in the corners, moved so the floors can be repainted.

Sorry, she says, unrepentantly. No, I'm not sorry. I'm the one who has to clean it up, anyway. Just don't step in it with bare feet.

She crosses her eyes at him, not that he can see that kind of detail from where he is. He springs up, jumps into the darkness. She hears his feet land with a solid thwack on the unforgiving ground.

She winces on his behalf.

That must have hurt, she says.

Are we just about done here? says X. It's late. I should be home for dinner.

He's pacing. She sees him pass somewhere below her, watches him disappear again.

Aren't you having fun yet? she says, pulling herself up higher and higher. She uses her most kittenish voice. Play with me, come on.

Yeah, sure, he lies. Fun. She can tell he's lying. He's as boring as Mira. Dull as her parents.

Hoisting herself up off the ladder, she pushes through an unlocked safety gate and ends up standing on the roof of a toy house. Boring. The plastic buckles a bit under her feet. She jumps experimentally, half-expecting it to crack.

Nothing.

She carefully slides off the roof onto one of the many bits of scaffolding that have been put up for maintenance crews. Then up the outside of the fake bakery and over the top. The plastic is stupidly slippery under her hard-soled shoes.

She kicks them off and watches them fall out of sight. She hopes she can find them later. From here, she can climb up and up and up. The highlight of the place is the suspension bridge, a rainbow of plastic encased in netting that's been partially pulled down for repair. The bridge goes from the village clock tower, which overlooks the shabby-looking houses and shops, to the flashy illuminated metallic and shiny disco ball of a castle. Like crossing the tracks, she thinks.

She gets to the bridge without following the kid route, the tunnels, which make her claustrophobic unless she's using them to get high. She can get to where she wants to go the hard way; it's better that way anyway. She can get there by climbing on the outsides of things. Slipping. Falling. Jumping. Swinging. Playing crazy chicken with herself.

When she was a kid, her parents had her in gymnastics and ballet and God knows what else. To "focus her energy," they said. She was the wild child. Mira didn't have to do that crap because she was born quiet and good. Don't want to put all that training to waste, Cat thinks, putting her hands on a barrier and scrambling over. Then, there she is, swinging above nothing, clinging to the net on the underside of the bridge. The concrete floor is a long way down. Too far. Vertigo wobbles through her, but she holds on tightly with her fingers, which suddenly feel not quite strong enough. She hooks her bare feet up into the net so she's stuck there like a sloth on a branch.

She can hear Robbo and Tic laughing from within one of the castle's turrets. Probably smoking up. Being jackasses.

Tic is cute, she thinks, closing her eyes so she can forget where she is. Robbo isn't. But still they look mostly the same, only Robbo is like an underexposed photo of Tic. Tic is made up of colours too garish and lines too sharp. Robbo is softer and blurrier and paler and less noticeable. The thing is that they are always together, so you look at both of them and then only really notice Tic.

Cat likes people who are noticed. She's noticed. X is noticed but that's because he's a tall black kid in a school of short white kids. Tic is noticed because he's *vivid*. Maybe she'll hook up with him. Maybe that's what she needs. Besides, it would probably shock X into realizing how much he probably actually likes her after all. *Loves* her even. Make *something* somehow change in how he feels, how she feels, how everything feels. Make it explode. Make it sharp and true and painful and real.

Hey, she says. X.

She can tell X is watching her, that his gaze is nervous. Well, good. She's nervous, too, but she can't stop herself.

You're an idiot, she says, loudly enough for him to hear. She's talking to herself, not to him, but he can't know that.

You're on your own, he says.

Not you, she says, but he's already shifted back and is moving away. He's inside a building, she can trace his progress through the tunnels. But it's confusing. Loud, quiet. She's disoriented. Is he coming closer or fading into the distance?

X? she yells.

X, c'mon, she shouts. She isn't sure now. Where is he?

He stands up and smashes what must be his head, swears loudly. He's close. Relief seeps through her like oil.

The sound of the plastic giving and bending under his weight is audible enough to make her feel okay. She wiggles a bit, gets some momentum and manages somehow to get herself swinging. Back and forth, back and forth. Just enough to convince herself that she isn't afraid. She's waiting for him, but she's not. What could he do, anyway? She'll have to get herself down somehow. No one could help her.

She moves her hands one at a time so she's a bit closer to the end of the bridge. Her upper body is strong, muscles like pebbles under her skin, hurting and shaking. She can tell that she's drunk because her arms and legs feel loose and detached, the trembling looks like it's happening to someone else. She makes herself look, lets her head drop down and back so she sees everything from upside down. If she fell right now, she thinks, she'd burst open like ripe fruit. And who would care? She frowns. Well, her mum and dad. Mira, probably. X? she guesses.

Out of nowhere, she is suddenly struck by a wave of remorse, of loss, of self-loathing. She wishes she had real, true girlfriends. A best friend. Not just boys who hang around her because they like her boobs and the fact that she looks like a slut. She can hear X's breathing, he's close enough to almost grab her. With all the strength she can tap into, she manages to pull herself all the way up, back over the rope safety net, onto the bridge. For a second, her toes are stuck, but then she's free. Just out of his grasp. The bridge sways under her weight.

This would be terrifying for a kid, she says out loud.

X is so close she can see him blinking. I guess, he says. I'm not liking it much either. Don't like heights. He laughs at this, like he's said something funny. She shrugs and stands, making her way slowly, slowly, slowly across the fifty or so feet of bridge to the castle. To the other side, away from him. The slats are wide, multi-coloured plastic. Shifty and slippery.

Ladies and Gentlemen, she says, once she's crossed, moved from inside the castle, up the trestle outside it and, through some feat of magic, pulled herself onto the outside. May I present the magical stylings of ... Cat! She claps for herself.

Don't kill yourself, calls X. She can't see him very well from where she is. He's lying down, it looks like: lower body on the bridge, upper body still on the floor of the tower it attaches to. Is he *stuck*? Is he really not going to come closer, not grab her, not stop her? Is he kidding? He's not much of a drinker, she thinks. This pisses her off. He's so *weak* and infuriating. There's no sign of the other two. No sound. Where did they go?

They're probably raiding the vending machine in the lobby, that's all. Probably up to something bad, but not too bad. Not like they're blowing the place up or something.

Undaunted by her apparent lack of audience, Cat steps onto a support beam that stretches from the castle to the warehouse wall. It's narrower and more sloping than she'd thought and it wobbles when she steps on it.

She bites her lip and looks over at X. Is he looking back at her? She can't tell.

She wishes she had a cigarette. She takes a few hesitant steps out onto the beam and twirls. Gaining confidence, shakily and slowly. Tentatively, she reaches down with her hands. It feels solid. Pretend it's a foot off the ground, she instructs herself, and then suddenly flips into a cartwheel.

That makes X look. It sounds klutzy. Her bare feet scrabbling for a grip on the plastic beam. Searching, searching, finding. Relief feels like strength flooding her.

Stop it, X calls.

She laughs. Her adrenalin is going nuts. Surging. It feels good. It makes her feel lucid and clear-headed.

Hey, she says. Six points from the German judge.

Get down, X says.

He's paying attention now, she thinks. Good. She stands there, arms above her head, thinking about what to do next. She can't tell from his tone whether he's imploring her or whether he's bored by the whole thing. Is he annoyed or afraid? She'd prefer afraid, given a choice. She wants to make him feel something.

Maybe I should run away and join the circus, she says. Only it comes out "shircus." She's drunk. She wobbles precariously.

You're being stupid, says X.

He looks pissed off.

Okay, I'll get down, she says. But first ...

And she bends backwards. She's thinking of doing a backwards walkover. She used to be able to do them in her sleep. When she was nine. She's not nine any more. Her centre of gravity is different. Alcohol rushes around in her blood.

Cat, she hears him scream, and then she's falling, backwards, falling for a long time. Hands stretched out and somehow — how? — X is holding her, somehow at floor level. They're on the castle drawbridge, the fake moat under them painted with alligators that seem to swim past her dizzy eyes. She clings to his neck and mumbles, Thanks, but she chokes on the word and it comes out as a cough.

It's only as they are driving home that she thinks, how the hell did that happen? It isn't possible. It was too far to fall and land without breaking bones, without damage. How the *fuck* did he do that? She's dizzy. She doesn't understand.

X won't meet her eye. Slams out of the car. Says, Good night, assholes. Disappears into his sad-sack little trailer. He has to duck to fit in the door.

I'm breaking up with him anyway, she tells Tic, who is staring at her from the back seat, his eyes wide and dilated.

Whatever, he says, patting her head limply. Nice haircut.

Yeah, she says, turning up the radio. Whatever.

Ruby

9

SOMETHING IS HAPPENING to you. You are stuck in a place between ennui and some sort of pain that is too scary to explore. Does something hurt?

No. Not literally.

But it's *something*. Something is changing. A constellation of acne has bloomed on your chin. You touch it now with your hand, gently. It stings. You've never had acne before, and it makes you want to scream and cry and hide your head under an old sack until it goes away. One thing you counted on about your appearance was your skin, your pale even skin. Now it, too, is letting you down. Red and angry.

Maybe you are red and angry.

I'm taking Cassidy on a holiday to that place where we went, says your dad. She needs a break. She's been working too hard. It's not good for anyone to never go on holiday. Would you believe she's never been away?

He's eating ice cream out of the carton, offering it to you like you'd want to share his slobbery spoon. You used to do things like that. Before.

I don't want any ice cream, you snap impatiently, spinning on your bar stool. Slowly. What place?

You know the place, he says. Storm watching. That lodge that has the cabin with the hot tub on the deck. He winks.

Is he demented? He winked at you? You're supposed to imagine Cassidy and your dad getting it on in the hot tub on the deck? You're supposed to ... what? Nudge him and make a face? Congratulate him? It's too disgusting to even contemplate. Is he so out of touch with you that he thinks this is the sort of banter he should have with you? You're his *kid*.

And the place. Well, it's *your* place. You swallow even though your mouth is dry. Your heart drops all the way to your feet and somehow, it relodges in your chest. Hammering.

The place at the beach? you say.

Yeah, he says. She'll like that, won't she?

Of course, you say, but it comes out more like "gorse." You nod vigorously.

Who wouldn't like it? You and your dad have been going there every winter forever, just for a weekend, to watch the huge waves crash along the West Coast in an array of wild spray and power. You've gone every year. Forever.

Forever, you say out loud.

What? he says. Are you sure you don't want some of this? It's so good. Your favourite.

You look at him blankly. It's not my favourite anymore, you say.

Your loss, he shrugs. He pats you on the head like a dog. Why can't he see that you're incandescent with rage? Is he stupid?

You and I will still go there, too, sweetness, he adds. It's still our place.

Uh, you say.

If there was ever a time when you could light a fire with your eyes, it's now. You stare hard at a piece of paper and will it to explode into flames, but, of course, it doesn't. Dumb. People can't light things on fire because they're in a bad mood, not psychically, anyway.

You sure you'll be okay on your own for that long? he asks, looking back at you over his shoulder. He's rinsing off the spoon before leaving it on the counter. They always leave an ice cream spoon on the counter, in case of sudden hunger. That's what he used to say: in case of sudden hunger. It was like a joke, your private joke. He dries the spoon and puts it away in the drawer.

Of course, you say witheringly. I'm seventeen, not seven. Go. Have fun.

Thanks, he says, as though he believes that you mean it.

You shrug and stomp as heavily as you can into your room, really heavy stomping being impossible because this apartment is so thickly, richly, well constructed that even stomping sounds like tiptoeing. Slam the door, which also doesn't slam, some kind of hinge causing it to settle into its frame like a sigh.

Well, fuck that, you think. Fuck you, Dad. FUCK YOU. Only you don't say it out loud. Instead, you flop face first into your pillow, your zits hurting against the rough cotton.

You want to scream.

Instead, you close your eyes. You breathe. You listen to the hushed sounds of your dad talking on the phone. To

Cassidy, of course. Explaining the romantic surprise. Closet doors open and shut: packing already. He's not leaving until Thursday, but he has to start now. He's overly organized, anal retentive, annoying in his planning carefulness.

You can hardly stand it. You can't explain it. You don't understand why you feel so totally destroyed. *Betrayed.* Cassidy in the hot tub on the front deck of the cabin, laughing in the moonlight. Of course, she should be. It's a romantic place. She's your father's girlfriend. You're his daughter. You shouldn't be in romantic places with him. There is something wrong with you that you're jealous.

You are sick.

For the next two days, you pretend to be normal. Your skin pustulates. You make jokes about your zits, and your father laughs and tells you that his zits were so bad he had to have surgery when he was grown up to reduce the pocking. This doesn't make you feel better.

It makes you even madder.

You don't say anything.

Finally, he leaves. He goes while you're at school, and when you get home, you know he's gone because his packed bag is missing from its perch by the front door, and there is a note on the counter that says, REMEMBER TO EAT NOTHING BUT ICE CREAM. VEGETABLES ARE FOR SISSIES! That's the kind of thing your father thinks is funny.

You crumple it up, throw it in the garbage and crawl into bed, even though you aren't sick. You're just empty. Empty empty empty.

You get up and make toast and eat it, your sheets filling with crumbs that scratch your skin. You eat a lot of toast.

You think about things you don't want to think about. For example, you think about your mother. You pull your favourite photo of her out of your school binder, where you always tuck it. In the picture, her mouth is half-open, and you can see her bottom teeth are very crooked. She's in the middle of saying something and she isn't smiling. In this picture, you think, she probably looks most like how she would normally look. In a lot of the pictures you have of her, she's smiling hard and you can tell that she never really looked that way. Most people don't.

You look at her picture. She looks like you, a bit, but mostly like herself. Her hair was messy, maybe being lifted by the wind, or maybe she had slept on it wrong and hadn't bothered to comb it. Was your mother the kind of person who didn't comb her hair? Are you?

You stop combing your hair. In fact, you stop washing your hair, and it gets progressively grosser until it looks dark with oil when really it's so blonde it's nearly white. This makes you look more like your mother.

That will show your dad how upset you are. Except it won't, because he won't see it.

You can't understand why you're so mad.

Even looking at the picture makes you mad. Once you showed it to Tic. To Joey. But you think of him as Tic when you remember the Picture Incident because he was such an asshole; he was like someone you didn't know. You know Joey. You don't know Tic. Anyway, you'd been talking about the fire, which Joey was always fascinated with. He can't believe you remember it and, for some reason, he loves to hear you tell the story. He makes you feel like you are telling the truth, that you do remember, that somehow this makes you special. After you told him the story, you pulled out the picture to show him. He was just looking at it, you can see it there in his hand, sitting on the falling down rock wall in the old park. It was sunny, the bright blue sky reflecting off his eyes. He was so beautiful you could feel a pang in your heart. He was looking at the picture when out of nowhere, X and Robbo appeared. The picture was in Joey's hand, Joey looking down at it and saying, Not much of a looker, was she? and it dropped in slow motion to the patchy grass below. There were cigarette butts there and a handful of tabs from the tops of cans, a crumpled bag of empty chips and a McDonald's fries box.

You felt like you'd been punched.

You remember now that X picked up the picture. Passed it to you. Glanced at it and said, Pretty. But he was just being nice. She wasn't actually very pretty. There's something wrong with that, as though, if you have a dead mother, she ought to have been very beautiful. Ethereal. Forever young and forever gorgeous. You snatched the picture back, didn't look him in the eye, although you could feel his eyes on you, his feeling sorry for you. This made you mad. You turned and walked away without another word to any of them, not to Joey, that's for sure. You were mad for weeks, but he didn't much notice.

The thing is that you think maybe that's what you like about him. Maybe you're used to being casually dismissed.

Your dad calls and you tell him that you're sick and once you've said it, it becomes true. It starts out with a hollow feeling in your throat, like it has been scooped out like ice cream. Turns into a low-grade fever. He says he'll send people to check on you, which makes you laugh out loud. Who? Why?

After you spend days lying on the sofa, watching TV, watching whatever is on, watching and not watching, feeling too down to even change the channel, the sickness forgets itself. It wasn't the sore throat that really got to you, it was something else. Something more global, bigger. Like you were being crushed under the weight of everything: oceans and forests and cities pressing down on your chest so heavily you could barely bother to breathe.

Eventually, the checkers check in: At your dad's request! they say brightly as they hover there, filling up the doorway. You think they are probably scrutinizing your ragged appearance, but you don't care. They all bring you food, like they would if someone had died. It's so awkward it's actually funny, the door buzzing and someone you don't even recognize thrusting a casserole dish toward you. How did your dad get the word out so quickly? Did he send a mass e-mail? My kid has the flu, take noodles, I'm too busy humping my girlfriend in the hot tub.

It's like a contest to see who can best feed the girl from the famous book. The really funny part is that you have about twelve casseroles stacked up in the fridge. You've had to take out all the condiments to make room. Which emphasizes to you that your dad has more friends than you do, which makes you feel much worse. How could one person — especially one sick person — eat so much in a handful of days?

Your skin is itchy and toast crumbs are beginning to leave a pattern of indents on your leg. You give in and have a bath. Change your clothes. Wash your sheets. Turn off the TV.

Lying in your bed at night, you are struck by the overwhelming impossibility of it all. How are you ever going to grow up? How will you ever go to college? How can you ever have a life and explain to anyone how you couldn't sleep until you heard the jangle of your father's keys, his deep, even breathing filling the apartment until it felt like home?

Finally, you force yourself to get on with it. Up at the normal time for school, have a shower — which in itself seemed almost impossible — you had to remind yourself about soap, shampoo, rinse, conditioner, rinse, all the complex steps that go into it. You get dressed, go outside, walk the mile to school. Now you're here and it's as dull as daytime TV. And as pointless.

You sigh and try to plaster an interested-in-what-you're-saying expression on your face. Mr. Beardsley is telling an anecdote in the same tone of voice that you would expect someone to use when talking to a coma patient. Hushed. Monotone. His voice is lulling you awfully close to the sleep that's been eluding you. To keep yourself awake, you gouge your pen into your palm over and over again, and when you look down, your hand is covered with blue dots. You hide it quickly on your lap. Stare hard at Mr. Beardsley and nod like you understand.

You look around. A handful of people are conspicuously missing: X. And Cat. You notice without really noticing. You notice how uncomfortable the chair is and you notice that your ink-smudged hand has left a blue mark on your khaki pants. You think about knitting. Your mother used to knit, apparently. Your dad told you in passing before he left. Maybe you should knit. Maybe she passed on to you some kind of magical knitting gene. You try to picture the kind of sweater you would knit yourself.

Bulky and beige, you think. Comfortable and thickly warm. You're staring into space, not thinking anything, when you realize you are staring at Joey, without meaning to. You feel defensive, you feel like saying, I was thinking about knitting! Not you!

He winks at you. You glare back. Had he even noticed that you were gone? That you were sick? He belches into his cupped hand and then waves his hand around like he's just performed an incredible party trick. Joanne, sitting on his left, giggles hysterically, but he ignores her. Staring at you. His eyes are so blue that they look like marbles. Glassy, too. He's probably baked. This makes you mad at him, even though he's always baked.

He throws his pen at you. You grab it and nod at him and half-smile, like you'd wanted his pen. You put it in your purse. Now he'll have to ask for it back. You know for a fact that he only ever has one pen.

It's really pretty sad that he's the closest thing you have to a friend. Other than Courtney and Joanne, but you don't care about them, so they don't count. They might want to be your friends, but you don't want them. Isn't that how life goes? The people you want don't want you, the wanters are unwanted. Courtney and Joanne, with their matching highlights and careful eye makeup and future plans. Well, they aren't like real friends, they're more like ... *accessories*. People that you wear so you aren't naked. Being alone makes you feel naked. When you are with them, you are properly hidden.

You don't really know anything about them.

You doodle your name in the margin of your notes. Some curlicues. A scribble that you colour in.

Psst, says Joey.

You don't turn around. You wish you didn't like him. Like him like that. You can tell he doesn't like you. But it doesn't stop you. You wish that his whisper didn't make you flush with happiness. You *really* wish you could get a crush on someone safe or someone more obvious. You cough. He coughs. You turn to glare at him again, but you feel like you're overacting your part. Your face reddens, no doubt making your pimples glow furiously under the fluorescent lights, and you look away. Cover your chin with your hand. You jot down in your notebook something that resembles something Mr. Beardsley is saying. Your pen is nearly out of ink, and the dry sound of the nib scratching the paper makes you shudder.

Shit, you think to yourself. You feel like screaming it.

Then you are interrupted from your anger as the door suddenly flings open and Cat lurches through. She can get away with that, you know it. Mr. Beardsley pauses, flinches, doesn't say anything. Cat takes her time getting settled, her books slamming against her desk. Everyone watches.

You catch her eye and she winks at you. You stifle a laugh. You want to laugh.

Maybe she knows, you think. Maybe she gets it, on some level. Maybe ...

Maybe not.

Cat leans back, like her desk chair is a lounge at the beach. Mr. B. starts talking again, stammering a bit. Cat starts gouging something into her desk with the back of her earring. From where you are sitting, it looks like an X. Of course, it's an X. She's X's girlfriend. Duh. Even Cat has a boyfriend. Pierced, weird Cat. And you don't.

You're too lethargic to do anything more energetic than watching the dust of fake wood falling to the ground beside her desk.

Your dad called last night to say he was coming on the morning flight. This morning. He's probably arriving now. He was bubbling over with an idea for a new "project," a thought that you find nearly unbearable. "Project" in his lingo means "book." What is he going to write about next? What more can he say about you?

In spite of that, knowing he is home is making you feel sleepy. He's probably there now. You hope the house-keeper got there first and cleaned up all the plates and dishes you left scattered everywhere. You hope she threw out all the casseroles.

You sigh noisily. You're hyperventilating, you can tell, but that doesn't stop you from continuing to sigh. You're feeling light-headed. You get into this weird thing where you have to yawn and sigh all the time. Your dad says it's classic hyperventilation syndrome. Anxiety, he says.

I'm not anxious, you tell him. I don't care.

Still, the symptoms fit his description. You feel like you are there, but not quite there. Like you are at a distance from yourself.

Mr. Beardsley drones on and on. It's like he's in a trance or something. Like he doesn't notice how no one cares. No one is listening.

Will he ever stop talking? you think. Fifty minutes can be forever.

You wake up when your head slams hard against your desk.

Shit, you say, this time out loud.

The bruise leaks across your forehead like ink dropped into water; you feel like you can actually sense it spreading. You grab your stuff and just leave, hurrying. Straight to the washroom, to a mirror, to inspect the damage. You see that the bruise somehow makes all your veins creepily hyper-visible. Like they were drawn onto your forehead with a blue ink pen. You comb your hair out of its ponytail and let it hang over your face. It doesn't look any better, kinked where the elastic held it together, crooked. But at least you feel a bit concealed. The bell goes and you hesitate. The idea of going to your next class seems like too much. You sigh again (don't hyperventilate, you remind yourself sharply), slide down onto the floor and just sit there, your hands resting on the cold tile.

You're so sleepy. Has it been a week since you've slept? Really slept? Or were you asleep the whole time?

You start to fade, and nearly jump out of your skin when the door swings open, barely missing your leg. Cat jumps over you and barely makes it to the toilet, throwing up like she's about to turn inside out. Your heart hammers in your throat, the loud sound of her seems like too much to bear.

Oh, God, you say, when she stops. Are you okay?

I'm fine, she says, eyes glittery. Sweat on her brow. You can see her annoyance. She doesn't like you, you think. You duck your head down. You were wrong. You'd thought there was a glimmer of something, but no. As usual, you imagined it. Like you imagine that Joey likes you back.

Hangover, she explains rudely. You know how it is.

She pushes past you to the sink. She puts her head right in it, gulping from the tap. Rinsing and spitting. You can't imagine doing that. You think, Germs. You think of all the filth.

Don't ... you start, but then remember it's none of your business and she doesn't like you, anyway.

She smiles at you vaguely.

Nice bruise, she says.

Thanks, you say. You want to say something else, but you don't.

You hate yourself for being intimidated by her. It's so stupid. You're so stupid. She leaves in a flurry of paper towel.

Fuck you, too, you say to her departing back.

Nobody really likes you.

Finally, you hoist yourself up off the ground. Your pants are damp. You feel filthy and disgusting, like the smell of Cat's vomit is clinging to you, even though it can't be. It didn't touch you. You're afraid of throwing up yourself. You hate that feeling so much, food punching at the back of your throat, like choking in reverse.

You shudder and push open the door. Fall back out into the stream of students moving from one class to the next. Let them envelop you.

I'm invisible, you tell yourself. And you reach up to press on the bump on your head because at least the part that hurts jerks you back into the moment. You can't slip away while it hurts.

X

10

I TRY TO swing the club with one arm. I remember that when I was learning this game, my old teacher showed me how you only need one arm to play. Your left. Your right hand just rests there, he said. The left does all the work. He had a drill that he used to make me do where I hit bucket after bucket with my left hand. I can't do it at all now. I'm all off-balance. Fuck it, I think. It's pointless, anyway. Why am I practising? I won't be in the tournament this weekend, that's for sure. The doctor says the cast will be on for twelve weeks. Twelve weeks is forever. I'm screwed. I'll be so out of practice by spring, there's no way I'll get scouted.

It's over. No golf scholarship for me. Makes it easy when your choices are narrowed, huh? Makes you realize what a great thing you just fucked up.

Thwack, I hit the club into the mat. Hard, jarring my left arm. The lady in the next cubicle misses her shot and says, Fuck.

You said it, I say out loud, and she looks over.

Broke your arm, huh, she says.

No kidding, I say.

She turns back to her game. She has her hair in one of those tight braids, I don't know what they're called. It's golden and shiny and swings on her back like a rope. She's pretty for an older woman. Half-heartedly, I line up a ball and try again, flinching when I hit the ground behind it instead. My left arm twinges. And it's not like my right arm doesn't hurt badly enough. In its big white fucking cast. I'm such an idiot.

I probably should have let her fall. That sounds so mean, but maybe she wanted to. Maybe she should have broken *her* arm.

I caught Cat. When she fell.

I didn't even feel it when the bone snapped, but I saw it on the X-ray. A clean line, like it was drawn there with a Sharpie.

I flew. I saw her start to fall, and I *flew*. I couldn't help it. I guess I am some kind of superhero after all. It was like instinct, like an animal. I flew before I thought of it myself, I was in the air before it occurred to me that I could do that. That I could save her that way.

The big fucking *punchline* of this great fucking joke is that I saved her life and she didn't even thank me. She didn't say anything, just kind of shook for a minute. Trembled. Reminded me of a kitten that we once found curled up in the heating unit of the trailer. You'd think it would've fried, but it didn't. Skinny and starving. We took it to the pound.

She should have fucking *said* something, that's all I'm saying. Acknowledged her stupid risk taking, fallen all over herself to apologize. Anything normal. Anything nice.

But no, not Cat.

After I caught her, she kind of paused and then pushed herself off me, like I was holding her back. All but fucking ran away. I guess what it comes down to is that she's the kind of person who just expects to be saved. Takes it for granted, like she's been caught for her whole life. She just expects someone to be there to catch her every time. I don't know if she saw me flying. Or felt it. I don't think she could have, because she would've said something. Wouldn't she have said something?

She must have felt it, though. That feeling of being lifted.

But if she did, would she think it was real? Or just part of her drunken haze, a blur of goings-on that happened while she was spinning colours in her head? I hate that she drinks. I hate that she smokes. I hate it all. Drunk girls are disgusting, and she was as drunk as she's ever been. I could tell by the way she flopped into me, loose limbed, bleary.

I'm such a selfish jerk that my first thought wasn't, Oh, good, I saved her. It was, What if someone saw me? Followed right away with, Way to be grateful, you bitch.

Aren't I nice? I'm a superhero with a chip on my shoulder. I'm a super-asshole.

Funny twist is that I didn't even know that my arm was broken until I woke up this morning and felt like I'd been hit by a fucking truck. It didn't hurt when it happened. How can that be? The doctors at the hospital said they couldn't believe I waited so long to come in. They didn't understand how I could not notice it until the morning.

I honestly didn't. I think it was all the adrenalin maybe. And the flying, well, it makes me feel both separate from myself and more a part of myself than ever, but it's like I'm disoriented from my body somehow. I just didn't feel the pain. Does that make sense?

Does any of this make sense?

I'm tired.

I'm so so so tired.

You know what I want? I want to go to your place, where you are, and just crawl into bed beside you. Not to jump you or anything, but just to lie next to you. How fucking lame does that sound? Not only does it sound like a horrible crime, it sounds disturbing. But I still want it. I can't understand it myself, so don't ask me to explain. It just seems like maybe that's the only place where I might be comfortable. I might be okay.

Maybe I'm just exhausted. That's why I'm talking crap, because of the fatigue, the kind that punches you in the head and forces you to lie down and sleep wherever you are.

I'm mostly just so tired of Cat and her stunts and her neediness and her pushing me away and her pulling me back and all her ... *stuff*. I'm tired of the way she always has to get attention. The way she pushes the envelope. The way she pushes *me*. Sometimes I feel like I've been married to her for twenty years and there's no way I can be free of her, then I think, *What*? I can dump her whenever I want. I *can* get away.

Then I want to go back and save her again.

Stupid, huh?

I'm so tired of her.

I guess if I hadn't caught her, maybe she would have died. It was a long drop and concrete doesn't make a soft landing, not even for me, especially with someone in my arms.

What was she thinking? I know she's wild, but I didn't think she was suicidal.

Ka-pow.

Ka-pow.

Thwap, I hit a good one, even though moving my body to do it feels like it takes every drop of energy in the world.

Nice one, says the lady next to me.

Thanks, I say. We both watch it vanish into the distance, me squinting, of course, and I can't really see it land. I try to do it again, and the ball wobbles off the tee and rolls about four feet.

Shit, I say.

Not your best, she says. Probably because I'm watching. I'm heading out, anyway.

See ya, I say automatically.

Yeah, she says, tossing her braid over her shoulder and lifting her clubs.

I hit a few more. I'm angry. My anger feels like hunger or something worse. Cramps in my belly. I never play well when I'm angry, even with two good arms.

In my head, I keep seeing Cat leaning over and pushing off into the blurry nothing below her. Laughing. Was she *laughing*?

She's crazy.

You know, I'd been there before, to that place. I didn't know that Troy was Cat's uncle; she never mentioned it, and I'm sure she knew that I took Mutt there last summer with some other kids from his playgroup. She always knows where I am. You'd think she would've mentioned it then, but she didn't. Those kids were cute, they really were. They called me Uncle Eggs. They were great. I even climbed around inside those stupid castles. Let the kids go down the slides. It's safe for kids, that place. But they stay *inside* the tunnels. They don't crawl around *on* them like jackasses.

I swing the club aimlessly. Whoosh. Whoosh. The feel of the air as it pushes past my body gives me a jolt of energy. A bit of a jolt, anyway. Enough to keep me awake. I don't even know why I'm still playing. It's just habit, I guess. Feels like something to do to get through my work shift. I always take an hour or so to practise.

I don't bother teeing up a ball. What's the point? It's freezing and the range is all but deserted. My arm is killing me. I'm obsessively thinking about the flying, the catching, the Incident, the moment when it could've all fallen apart. The truth is that I'm fucking terrified.

If I get caught, then what?

What happens next? To me? To anything?

To be honest, I'm freaking the fuck out.

I force myself to hit more balls, fall into the rhythm. The safe rhythm of golf.

Golf is safe. Golf is good. It's easy. It's *Zen*.

What if Cat says something? What if she tells? Then what?

What if she doesn't remember?

What if she does?

That's it, my biggest fear. It makes bile rise in the back of my throat, and I nearly throw up, right there on the practice mat. The big "what if": What if I have to *explain*?

I can't.

I feel like a freak. Like my heart's beating wrong, like I'm breathing wrong, like I'm moving wrong, swinging wrong. I'm out of sync with myself, with everyone, with the whole world.

I guess maybe I AM a freak. I'm a *huge* freak, and if anyone finds out they'll probably take me away somewhere. And do what, I don't know. I picture it like a bad science fiction film, electrodes on my head, some kind of cage. Dumb, I know. But I don't want that. I don't even want to be able to fly. I don't want the *responsibility* of it. I don't want any of it.

I'm so angry with Cat. I'm so angry. Like she's playing with me somehow. Breaking up, getting back together. It's like she's not even my friend anymore. She'd sell me out for almost anything, if she could get something out of it. She would. She'd tell. I don't know how I know, but I do. That's just who she is. She's someone who sprays the messy truth out there for everyone to see, fuck the consequences. Fuck everyone. That's Cat. She's feeling something, whatever it is, and BAM. Everyone wears it.

I hit another ball and then, for good measure, I smash the club against the ground a few times. The grass is frozen as hard as steel and the blades snap. I do it again, too hard. The head breaks off my club, my favourite driver. Deer's gift to me. It was expensive. Too expensive. I know she saved for ages. I almost start crying.

Great, I say to myself. I'm a big fucking baby.

Pack it up, Tiger, Bob says. Sneaking up behind me. A cigarette dangling wetly off his lower lip, smoke curling up into his nose like hair. We're closing up for the night. No one's going to play in this weather. Looks like we're going to get some serious snow.

Yeah, I say.

How's your arm? he says.

Broken, I say.

Yeah, he says.

Sometimes it freaks me out to think that I've known Bob since I was nine. Come to think of it, he's the closest thing to a father figure that I've ever had. I slowly walk up the row of stalls, picking up the few tipped-over buckets that are being blown around by the wind. I'm shivering in the icy blast of winter, and when I shiver, my arm tenses up and hurts like anything. An unreachable itch is starting deep under the cast.

Suddenly, there is nothing I want to do more than to go home to Deer and Mutt. I want to crawl into the warmth of the trailer. Have some tomato soup from a can, and maybe some toast and a hot shower. Crawl onto the couch, under a quilt. Watch the Golf channel. I stretch, careful not to move my broken arm. I keep thinking that I smell Cat's beery sweat on me, which isn't possible, but I still get wafts. It makes me gag as I bend over to straighten the last of the mats.

I'm headin' out, calls Bob, raising his hand to wave.

Later, I call.

Don't forget to lock up, he says.

I never forget, I yell.

Yeah, he says. Bye.

I wait until he's gone, and then I go into the office. Straighten up the papers that are slipping off the desk. Dump Bob's coffee cup into the sink. Flip the lights off. I reach for the phone to call Cat, and then I change my mind. I dial her number but hang up before the last digit. I don't know what I'm going to say. Maybe I'm going to break up with *her*. Make it official.

I don't know. I sit there for a bit in the dark, listening to the wind making shapes in the trees outside.

I put the broken head of my Big Bertha in my pocket. Maybe one of the guys in the shop can fix it for me tomorrow. And then I run — okay, I fly, but real low so it looks like I'm running — home across the cow field. It's getting easier to do this. It's getting to be more natural, feel more right. My feet skim the tops of wet shrubs, the wind pushes me faster.

Even the cows aren't stupid enough to be out on a night like tonight. I don't go directly home. It's dark, no one is out. My wings unfold like something I'm remembering from a dream I had a long time ago. It's so strange. I'll never get used to it. I fly up into the night, higher than I've dared to go before. I feel like I should do this while I can. I've suddenly got the idea that this isn't going to last. That whatever it is is as temporary as love and all that other fleeting garbage that we think is true. Hell, even life is temporary. Everything is. I go up and up and up and float back down again. Getting braver. I go so far up that the street lights are just tiny dots beneath me, I could fold my wings up and impale myself on them as mysteriously as anything.

What would people think when they found me?

I go so high that my head gets light, and I think about what would happen if this gift or whatever it is went away just then and I fell to the earth. I'm afraid of heights, so that's the worst thing I can imagine: falling. But I still do it. It's like the fear is all wrapped up in the flying, and I can't separate them, and I'm starting to like it more and more, which scares me sick. It does. I wonder how far into the earth I'd go if I fell. Who would find me. What would they think I'd fallen from?

I read once that when angels fall, they get to be human. That's fucking stupid, I know. Who believes in that crap? I don't.

I don't know what I believe anymore.

I am flying by the building where you live. Red brick on the outside, lots of glass so shiny it's a mirror. Can you see me? I want to ...

I don't know.

I want to fly right into your window and talk to you. I feel like you would understand, but maybe you wouldn't. Maybe you'd just be afraid. I don't know. I think that I think I know you but really I don't have a clue. I have a crush. That's all. I think you're special because I have a stupid crush on you, and maybe you're not. Maybe you're just ordinary. I don't know.

I don't know much of anything. I wonder how high I could go, if I could just keep going, if I'd eventually burn up in the atmosphere like a meteor. I guess it would get really cold up there. The wind is making me feel like I couldn't possibly fall. It's underneath me, like a floor that no one else can see. I fly fast. It feels wrong to do this, to spy on you or spy near you or any of that. To see you when you can't see me.

I turn around. I spin. I *swoop*. I go right past your window, so close I can see you. I can *see* you.

Crazy.

My arm pulses with pain. I turn for home.

At least my wings aren't broken, I guess. At least that's one good thing.

CA✝

II

CAT WISHES SHE *had* died. It's all a blur, anyway. She can hardly remember what happened, building up to the fall. When she tries to think specifically about it, her knees weaken, sweat springs onto her palms. She's so stupid she doesn't deserve to live.

Besides, if she'd died, then she wouldn't feel like she feels right now. Even after a whole day of throwing up, she still feels like shit. Like her body wants to turn inside out. To make matters worse, she must be premenstrual. Her breasts hurt and she feels like crying. She told her mum she had the flu. Her mum said, Doesn't smell like the flu.

So she's caught. Drinking on a school night. Drinking and driving. Her ugly car taken away forever probably. She rolls over onto her back and scowls hard at the ceiling, willing it to burst into flames like in a Stephen King novel, or crack open, or liquefy. Willing it to collapse.

Something big.

Something dramatic.

She'd kill for a cigarette, but she doesn't have any and can hardly get up and take the *bus* to the only store where they'll sell her some. Taking the bus to school in time for afternoon classes was bad enough. Horrible. All those vinyl seats and stinky people. She gagged at least three times. And when she finally got to school, she caught a whiff of someone's tuna fish sandwich in the hallway and threw up in a potted plant. Embarrassing. Humiliating. Even though it was more dry-heaving than actual puke.

She flings an arm over her head. Wonders why X hasn't called. Maybe he didn't go to school either. Maybe he's hungover, too. Probably. He'd better be.

Was he drunk?

She certainly fucking hopes so. So he doesn't remember too much. So he doesn't remember how she threw up in her shoe. How she swerved home. She hopes ...

Well, who cares what she hopes?

She thinks about calling him but can't be bothered to get up and find her cell phone if it even still works. She hasn't used it for days, loses it all the time. Cell phones are a pain.

She can hear Mira in the next room, busy fingers clattering away on the keyboard like rats' feet in the attic. Mira is writing a book, unbelievable as that sounds. Some goody-goody suck-up book for children about saving the planet or the whales or the wildebeests or some such shit. Mira calls it a "story," but it's already about a thousand pages long. Cat's seen the neat, scary-big pile of paper building up in the box next to Mira's desk. Knowing Mira, by next year it'll probably be a 20th Century Fox movie starring the drunk, partying starlet of the moment or some kid who has divorced his parents. That's the kind of luck Mira has.

Cat gets off the bed and goes and gets her sketch pad and starts redrawing her design for the X tattoo. She's going to have to get it done professionally because she asked Mira and Mira laughed. No way, she'd said. Not on your *life*.

Her hand pushes too hard on the pen, tears through the paper like it's used Kleenex. She chews on the pen lid, flips the page and starts the design again on a smooth new sheet, this time using a charcoal pencil stub she finds on the floor. It's smoother and doesn't bug her the way pen-on-paper scritching bugs her. Makes all her hair stand on end. She puts her headphones on and tries to listen to music, but she can still hear the sound of Mira's typing, making it impossible for her to concentrate. It's like claws clattering in her brain.

She breathes in furiously, pretending to smoke. Fuck, she says and gets up. Dumps her purse out looking for cigarettes or something to take her mind off this nausea and this headache. She pounds on the wall.

Keep the fucking noise down, she yells.

A minute later, Mira is in the doorway. What noise? she says.

You were typing too loud, Cat growls.

Mira laughs. That's crazy.

Whatever, says Cat.

Hey, says Mira. Hesitating. Then coming in and sitting down gingerly on the edge of Cat's bed. As though Cat's bed is covered with aggressive germs that might get her and turn her into a loser like her sister if she comes closer.

It's not catching, says Cat. It's a *hangover*.

I've never had one, says Mira speculatively. Looks painful.

Of course not, says Cat scathingly. It is fucking painful.

She bites her nails and glares at her sister. Anything else I can help you with, or did you just come in here to stare and gloat?

Mira shrugs. Wanted to know ...

What? says Cat. Wanted to check up on me?

She knows she's being mean; she just can't help it.

No, says Mira. It's not that. But if you're going to be a bitch, I'll go. I wanted to know if you were okay.

Don't go, says Cat. Forget it.

She doesn't want to be alone. She wants to tell Mira about how she fell and X caught her, but she doesn't.

How's old what's-his-pickle? she asks.

You mean, Nathan? says Mira. He's fine. I mean, he's good. He's fine, really. I'm sure. I mean, I haven't talked to him today.

Huh, says Cat.

You don't like him, do you? says Mira.

I don't *know* him, says Cat. And let's face it, we don't really have the same crowd of friends. My friends are stupid drunks and yours are ... well, like Nathan.

Yeah, says Mira. I guess. He's good-looking, isn't he?

I guess, says Cat. If you go in for that sort of thing.

I guess I do, says Mira. It's just that sometimes, honestly? I want to mess him up. You know? I want to make him less ... well-pressed.

Huh, says Cat. Don't blame you. He looks like he irons his head.

Mira laughs. Cat joins in. Really laughing. Belly laughing.

He probably gets his mum to iron it for him, sputters Mira.

Or the butler, says Cat.

But ... says Mira.

But what? says Cat.

I don't know, says Mira. He seems like a decent guy.

Yeah, says Cat, not laughing anymore. I'm sure he's fucking lovely. He's going to be what, a doctor? A lawyer? I'm sure you'll be really happy together.

Cat, says Mira. I'm not marrying him. I don't even know if ... well, if we're like dating, or what.

Dating, says Cat. She rolls her eyes. Lovely. What year is it in your world? 1950?

Don't be a bitch, says Mira. You really ... You have to ... I think ...

She stands up, straightens her shirt. Forget it, she says. I should get some more work done.

Whatever, says Cat.

Mira is standing in the doorway. She hesitates. Turns back. You know, she says.

What? says Cat.

Mira clears her throat. Touches her face, like she's nervous. You know, she starts again. It gets boring.

What does? says Cat.

You, says Mira. Your whole shtick. Your whole ... mean "thing." It's starting to be ...

What the fuck are you talking about? growls Cat. Her head is spinning a bit. She lies back down and closes her eyes.

Mira's voice gets louder. The whole "bitch" thing, Cat. The whole way you treat people, the way it's all "whatever" and no one matters. The way you hurt everyone and everything and act like everyone owes you something because you're pissed off.

She stops for a breath.

Fuck you, mumbles Cat.

You're a selfish, egocentric, self-centred bitch, Cat, finishes Mira. And I'm almost done with it.

She slams the door. The air vibrates. The room is still slightly spinning. Cat's dehydrated, she knows it. She should drink some water. Lots of water. Endless water. She pictures a waterfall of water pouring onto her face. Choking on it. Drowning.

She could drink a gallon of water and still feel like shit. Mira's right. She's a bitch. She's unredeemable. Her own sister, whom she figured would always be there, no matter what, apparently hates her.

Great.

Just fucking great.

She starts to cry, but crying hurts too much. Fuck it. She should quit drinking; it makes her feel terrible. It makes her an idiot, makes her cringe to see herself in the mirror. More so than when she's not drunk, anyway. Makes her whole self feel just generally *worse*.

Makes what Mira said, what she *ranted*, seem true.

She throws the pencil down and chucks the sketch pad on the floor. It's futile. She'll never get this tattoo. What she should do is split up with X. Let him go. Maybe she should have an affair with Mr. Beardsley. Yeah. That would shake things up a bit, wouldn't it? Yesterday, she brushed by him in the doorway and she could feel his attention on her. If she'd beckoned, he would have followed. She owns him. Cat laughs. It would be so easy, she thinks. And he's not bad looking. He's dull as anything, but that doesn't mean much. Maybe outside of the classroom he's a fireball.

Maybe.

Cat drags herself off her bed and fishes around on the floor until she finds a messy pile of college applications. She flips through the glossy magazines half-heartedly. Just looking at the pictures of the campuses makes her want to laugh. Or cry. She would never fit in there. Never, never, never. What a joke. She starts filling out the first application but gets stuck on the part where you have to fill in the address of your high school. She could look it up, but she can't be bothered. It just feels like too much. Even the application has a smell that alarms her. A clean, ink smell that gets into her nose and makes her feel ... inadequate. And nauseated.

Her skin feels all wrong. Uncomfortable. She gets up, looks outside — wintry, frigid, unforgiving. Presses her face against the glass to feel the slap of cold. Flops back down onto her bed, the tangled, sweaty sheets smelling musty and old. She tries to empty out her mind. Tries to forget how she felt, for that split second, like falling was the right thing to do. Like she was ... relieved.

She falls asleep that way, her arm flung up over her head like she's about to take hold of some kind of trapeze, about to swing herself out into the ether.

Ruby

12

YOU HAVE HAD six conversations with Joey in the past two days. It's intensifying your feelings for him a thousand-fold. It's his eyes. Not just that they are so intensely blue but that when he smiles, they scrunch up and his whole face smiles. His whole body. You can tell he's smiling even if you can only see the back of his head. His whole being smiles. It's that smile — in spite of all the stoned stupidness he often spouts forth — that makes your heart beat faster, literally. He gives you a racing heart.

This morning he touched your arm while he whispered an insult about the vice-principal in your ear. You think he said, Hey, it's hairy balls. (The VP's name is Harry Baker, so the joke itself was dumb, but it didn't matter.) Just that Joey was talking to you in school, in front of everyone, made you feel okay. Made you feel like you fit in, you belonged, you were in the club. You laughed and he repeated his joke out loud, to uproarious laughter from Robbo, who nearly bowled you over with his fake guffaw, complete with bending at the waist and flailing his arms. Robbo really

doesn't have many redeeming qualities, you think to yourself. He doesn't have the smile. He doesn't have the eyes. He
doesn't have the quick wit either. No matter how asinine
Joey is, he's still funny, even when it's lame.

Tic, he yelled. You're such a scream. You're a RIOT!
You are the FUNNIEST JACKASS IN SCHOOL!

And then they took off, laughing and punching each
other, down the hall, like Siamese hyena twins.

It was enough, though, to make your morning okay. To
make your morning good. It makes a difference: whether
you see him or not. Like yesterday, when Joey cornered you
in the elevator and got you to come up to the roof with
him. Got you to listen while he talked about how he was
freaking out about graduation. Freaking out about next
year. He talked — well, mostly rambled — for the better
part of an hour, and you basked in it.

Maybe, just maybe, he likes you.

Maybe it's real, after all.

You wander down the hall, dazed, toward your locker
where you have an apple or something. Something you
can eat, even though you forgot your lunch. You were
distracted. Like now, too distracted to notice Courtney
and Joanne descending on you. They're buzzing. You find
a day-old yogurt — how gross is that? — in your back-
pack. Probably the locker is cold enough that it's pretty
refrigerated. You allow them to sweep you up. Not for the
first time, you wonder why they picked you to be friends
with. What do they get from you? Nothing. You don't
share anything, you don't invite them places, what do they
want? Some droplet of fame? Well, you don't have any
of that to hand out. It's not yours to give. Or to have. You
don't want it, why would they?

They drag you over to their table in the cafeteria, where they chatter at you while you spoon the off-tasting yogurt mechanically into your mouth. It takes you a while to catch on to what they're talking about and then you realize that there is some kind of dance coming up. A Christmas Ball. Inwardly, you roll your eyes. High school dances. It hurts you to even think about them. The horror of lining up in the gym in over-the-top dresses, staring at each other. High heels on the lacquered floor.

It's just not you.

You open your laptop and wait while the word processing program opens.

Hey, says Courtney. Don't do homework, we want to talk.

You hate dances, because, let's face it, no one ever wants to dance with you.

I'm not going to the dance, you say, scraping the last of the raspberry stuff from the bottom of the container into your mouth. Typing into your computer with the screen angled away from them. You type, I'm not going to the dance.

You have to go, says Courtney. It's going to be fun.

I hate dances, you say. And then you type it.

No, you don't, she says. No one does. What are you writing?

I'm doing my homework, you lie. You type, I'm doing my homework.

Yeah, Joanne chimes in. It will probably suck but it might be fun. What would you rather do? Stay home and watch TV?

She laughs, so you join in.

No, you say, I guess not. Joey Ticcato, you type. Then you delete it quickly, blushing.

What you'd really like to do is go to the dance with Joey like a normal couple. Like two people who can be seen together out in public. The fact that he's too embarrassed to do anything like that makes you feel funny inside, like you've been caught out doing something humiliating when, really, his issues are nothing to do with you. He's *shorter* than you, and a *druggie*. What do you care? You lean forward. Okay, you say. I guess I can go.

Of course you can, says Courtney. Let's go shopping this weekend. Bring your dad's credit card. We can get some stuff to wear.

Sure, you say.

Your dad gave you a credit card on your sixteenth birthday, shiny, gold. It's like something you don't want to touch. I trust you, he said. *You'd* never take advantage of it.

In the past year, you've probably spent less than $500 on the card. You've bought sensible things like school supplies. You've used it to pay for his dry cleaning when he asks you to pick it up. You've bought Chinese takeout and pizza and green curry from that Thai place downtown. You've never once used it for anything crazy. Never once bought something you thought he'd disapprove of.

You roll your head around until your neck cracks definitively. Drag yourself back to the conversation.

Blah blah blah dance blah blah blah.

Courtney has drawn a butterfly on the back of her left hand with a red Sharpie. It looks like the distended rear-end of a monkey in season, which you saw in a Biology film two weeks ago. You laugh out loud, covering your mouth. Turning it into a choking fit, which becomes real, your windpipe closing, and you forget how to get the next breath until you remember again.

Courtney shoots you a funny look, but doesn't stop talking. She talks like an AK-47, ratatatatatat.

You nod at her, then type: I think my father is in love with Cassidy, and I think she wishes I didn't exist. When she looks at me, she looks like she's assessing an enemy. I think I feel jealous because he has time for her and not for me. I think she feels jealous that he writes about me and spends his days talking about me, all about me me me, but not with me. There's nothing to be jealous of with that.

Hey, says Joanne. You writing a book?

Huh? You say, slamming the computer shut. Nothing, you say. What?

Earth to Ruby, says Courtney. Come in, Ruby.

I'm listening, you say. I just had to write something for History before I forgot. Nothing personal.

Courtney leans over and whispers something in Joanne's ear, and they both laugh. You pretend not to care. You let your eyes drift around the room, unfocused, like the cluster of people might blur into the shape of a sailboat or a car if you relax your muscles just enough, like those pictures that look like dots until you cross your eyes.

Everyone's eating or shouting or both. It's so loud. Sometimes it's so noisy in the cafeteria, you think you could probably shout obscenities at people and no one would notice — or hear you, for that matter. Drift, drift.

For a second, your gaze locks with X's. He's sitting at the next table over. He's staring in your direction. You turn to look behind you, to see who or what he is looking at like that.

You.

He's definitely looking at you. There is nothing behind you to see, unless he's staring at the brick wall.

He smiles. You frown. Look down and away, don't let your eyes attach to his gaze. It feels like a trap. His smile wigs you out for some reason. There's something about him that is unsettling. You don't know what it is. He looks at you the way Mr. Beardsley looks at Cat. Maybe that's it. Like he wants you in a way that you don't feel like you want to be wanted.

I'm not ready for you, you telescope to him with your eyes, then you blush. What kind of thing is that to think? What's wrong with you?

Maybe you just don't like being stared at like you're a meal and he's hungry. You shiver, pull your sweater closer around yourself. It seems lately that you're always cold. A lump forms in your throat.

You cold? asks Joanne.

I guess, you say. Look, I've got some stuff to do for my next class. I should go do it.

Before they can stop you, you stuff your laptop into your bag and push past them and grab your books from your locker and go sit in the library. Instead of doing any work, you doodle on the page. Stupid stuff. Hearts. Your last name with Joey's. Then you scribble that part out hard with thick black pen that smells like something that shouldn't be legal, something that could make you high. You hold your breath.

You start over, staring at the Math problems that you really don't have to do until tomorrow. If a plane going 150 miles an hour, blah blah blah.

You don't know what's wrong with you lately, you just can't concentrate. You put your head down and close your eyes just for a minute. Just long enough for the fire dream to start. Just long enough that you wake with a start when the bell goes, sweat trickling down your forehead. It's stupidly unsettling to have your home nightmare out of context like that. It's like your nightmare has followed you to school, like some kind of stray dog. But it's all wrong and in the wrong place and time and it makes you feel dizzy and sad.

You decide not to go to class. Instead, you walk through the empty corridor, your sneakers squeaking on the floor. You eavesdrop on the classes through the closed doors, standing and listening here or there. Through the glass windows, you can see students slumped disinterestedly in their seats. It must be the weather, you think. Everyone is bummed. Dragged out. Sleepy. You keep walking until you get to the door that goes to the basement. You don't know why, but you go down there. It's warm and bright, not like what you would imagine. There are a bunch of boxes down there. You don't know what's in them. There are racks of clothes that the drama department uses for costumes. You go over and start flipping through them. A bunny costume. An Alice dress. A maid's outfit. It looks like a porn shop, you think, and then you laugh. Your laugh sounds too loud in the empty room, like a rooster. It startles you. You put your bag down and crouch down, like suddenly someone might see you. You might get caught. But caught doing what? Your heart is beating hard, like you're doing something really seriously wrong, not just cutting class. You're in an area that's off limits, too. You're looking at things you shouldn't see. You close your eyes.

There, you say. There.

After a few minutes, you get up and go back to the costumes. A king and queen outfit. Something that you think is supposed to be an oyster. A bunch of gypsy dresses. Upstairs, you can hear the bell go again and the sound of thundering footsteps in the hallway, a cacophony of raised voices. A door slams.

The door to the basement.

Shit, you think, shit shit shit. You grab your bag and hide behind a bunch of boxes. You can hear voices. One of them is Joey's.

I don't know, Tic, you hear Cat say. I broke his fucking arm. He hates me.

He doesn't hate you, says Joey.

Yeah, he does, says Cat.

You feel stupid hiding from them, but you can't let them know that you're here now. It's too late to pop up, act surprised, act casual. You hold your breath so they don't hear you breathing. You make yourself disappear.

No, he doesn't, says Joey. You just broke his arm and it hurts. He's in a pissy mood. Don't worry about it.

You hear the sound of matches striking and the sound of cigarettes being smoked. You smell it. You hope it doesn't trip the fire alarm or anything. Then you'd get caught for sure.

I'm breaking up with him, anyway, says Cat.

So you keep saying, says Joey.

Yeah, says Cat.

You close your eyes and will them to leave. Leave, leave, leave, you repeat to yourself. Go already. They are quiet for a while and you are just about to think that maybe they have left, when you hear Cat say, So, do you like me?

And you hear Joey say, Yeah.

You hear the sloppy sound of tongues and lips. Horrible, too loud, awkward. You don't want to know it, to hear it, to feel the sinking in your chest like it's collapsing.

Oh no, oh no, oh no.

After what feels like forever, they finally leave. Laughing and talking like nothing happened. You bitch, you're thinking. Not Joey. You have X. And Mr. B. And whoever you want. Not Joey.

You hate her. It takes you a while to stop crying, but when you do, you just want to get out of there, so you do. You just walk out of the school and get on the next bus, dumping handfuls of change — probably too much — into the bin. Hurtling yourself onto the last seat and slumping down so low you can't see out the window even if you wanted to look back. You never want to look back. You straighten up as the bus turns the corner and the school vanishes. You exhale on the window and draw a heart with your initials on it and then you rub it out.

You head home, stepping over homeless people in the doorway. Avoiding eye contact. Push open the front door, into the elevator, *finally* home. You can breathe now. You can sleep.

But no.

Cassidy is there. By herself. She is wearing your father's dressing gown. Drinking coffee and reading the paper.

What are *you* doing home? she asks you, as you are saying, What are *you* doing here?

Forget it, you say. You can't even summon the energy to try. You slam into your room and shut the door. Lock it. Throw yourself onto your bed, too feathery quilt around your face, suffocating. And you think, Now what?

X

13

EVERY NIGHT AFTER work, on days that I work, I fly home. Low to the ground at first, but I'm getting braver. I think that if someone sees me, they'll think they couldn't have seen what they think they saw, that I'm just walking fast or running smooth. I think their disbelief protects me somehow from getting caught. But "getting caught" sounds wrong. I'm not committing a crime. I'm just being different. Being different is not wrong.

But it is. That's the kind of fucked-up world we live in. Who am I kidding? It's totally wrong.

There's a building across the street from yours. It's grey, concrete, empty. There's a broken window on the third floor where the smashed-in glass is the exact shape of someone's head in profile. It's the kind of building that has to be haunted, the ghosts stuck in there like prisoners serving a life sentence for something they didn't do, or don't remember.

I land on the roof and from there, I can see into your apartment, lights all on. It's the tidiest place I've ever seen.

It's like a model of an apartment, like a kid would imagine a fancy apartment to look like if he'd never seen one. There's nothing extra anywhere, no sloppy art or clothes heaped on the floor. It's scary clean, like a display case at the museum.

I want all of this to not sound as messed up as it does. I'm not watching you. Not really. This is just the only abandoned building in town. This isn't a city where buildings are left to fall over, you know that. There must be a story behind this one, I just don't know what it is. I've been exploring a bit. It's an old old place. I wish I could say I found, like, treasure maps or some shit. Ghosts or old diaries. But what I mostly found was drug paraphernalia. Needles and smashed bottles.

Depressing.

Up on the top floor though, there's a bathroom with the most incredible mosaic tile on the wall. I wish you could see it. Well, maybe you have. I don't know. It's like your neighbour, although I doubt you do much crawling around in empty crack houses.

Sometimes, I glimpse you through the window. It's not even like I really mean to, not like I'm looking, but just kind of like I'm saying "hi" in my own fucked-up way.

I'm so going about this the wrong way, I know it.

Yeah, I'm sure I don't have the gift of flight so that I can *spy* on people. But I can't see that far, anyway, not far enough to actually catch any details of your life. I just like to see your lights on. Shit. You must think I'm really awful. I *feel* awful, yet I can't stop. It's like I'm hungry and there's no food, so I keep trying.

Or maybe I'm just an asshole.

Yeah, I think we're clear on that at this point.

I fly so close to your window, it's crazy. What am I doing? It's like I want you to look up and see me. You are looking hard at yourself in the mirror, close. Then I see what you're doing, you're flossing your teeth. So intently, like you can't stand the feeling of whatever is stuck between your teeth. Right away, seeing that, I feel sick and monstrous and awful. It wasn't anything. I mean, it's not like you were naked or anything like that. But I don't know. I saw something I shouldn't. That was your private place and I shouldn't have been there. I hated myself for a second. Pointed my feet and went straight down, past all the windows, not caring who else saw me.

I made myself walk home. It took an hour.

I guess that a part of me thinks that if I do get caught, at least you'll be forced to notice me. But not like that. I don't want you to notice me noticing you doing something personal, you know? I don't want it to be rude.

I saw you today in the cafeteria. I was staring at you, I guess, thinking about something else. But when your eyes caught mine, you flinched so hard you must have got whiplash, and you looked away. I know I'm ugly, okay? Do I scare you or something?

I just can't help looking at you. I try to stop, but I can't. Sick.

I'm sort of observing you, the way Cat observes stuff she thinks is ugly-pretty, like old beer cans smashed in the gutter reflecting light in some certain way, water beading off them. Not that you're like an old beer can, but you know what I mean. I'm not saying *you're* ugly-pretty. You're just ... pretty.

I think you get it, anyway, don't you? I don't know why I think that. Like you're going to save *me* or something. Somehow.

I heard you talking to Joanne and what's-her-name about the dance and for a second, I was ... I don't know. Excited, I guess. I got this idea that maybe we could dance together. Dumb. It's like I'm twelve or something and just got hormones and we're off to the sock hop. My friends would laugh their asses off to hear me say shit like this, that's for sure.

Everything's so crazy lately, it hardly seems to matter. It's like I'm thinking in poetry while my life is more like a WWF wrestling match. All glitter, all crap.

Mutt was drawing on my cast with crayons this morning while I tried to sleep in. That smell of crayons. Crazy. It always makes me think of kindergarten. Think of all that kid stuff that one day you just stop doing, you know?

Mutt wakes up every morning at five o'clock. It's still dark outside when he thump, thump, thumps out of bed, runs around the room, looks at stuff. I was still so tired that I let him keep drawing. He's drawn a bunch of brightly coloured scribbles and some things that might be people. They have orange heads and purple bodies. There are some blobs at the bottom near my wrist that look like eggs.

Deer is worried. I guess so. I mean, I know I'm going to miss this big tournament this weekend. Obviously. I can't play with one arm. And she's pissed or hurt — same thing — that I broke the Big Bertha. I am, too. It was my club. I'm the one who won't ever be able to afford another one.

Secretly, I wonder if I need another one. Is golf really going to be my life?

Golfing for a living means leaving. Leaving Deer. Leaving Mutt. What would Mutt do without me? I mean, I'm enough older than him that I'm almost like a dad, right?

Whenever I'm at home in that trailer with them, I think about how much space my leaving would leave behind. And it's too much.

But I think I know I can't stay there forever or for much longer. It's too small, anyway. Like, literally too crowded.

Cat's plan is to run away. Not that it's actually "running away" after you've graduated. It is before, but not after. After, it's just "leaving." When she told me, her voice had that dangerous laugh behind it. She said it like it was true, and I think maybe it is. She's going to go — or she thinks she's going to go — to New York. Become a rock star or a photographer or a God-knows-what. I wish I was brave like that, but the truth is that I'm not.

I'm just not.

You probably have a plan. You look like someone who has it together, who really knows stuff. Not like me. Not like Cat. Not like anyone else I know.

This morning, while I was eating, Deer said, I guess this means you're giving up, right?

I've never seen her so sad. I don't *want* to make her sad. How can I make her dreams come true and still figure out what my own are?

Of course not, I told her.

I wish you wouldn't hang around with that Cat, she said. She's bad news. I've got a bad feeling about her.

No kidding, I said. She's a bad-feeling kind of person.

Cat's still sick, days later. I can't believe it. She must have been drunker than I thought. Must have had alcohol poisoning to still be feeling the effects. How drunk was she and how could it have happened? Wasn't it just beer?

I keep seeing her falling and falling and falling.

The rooftop is gravelly under my hands, I crouch down and feel it. Just to remind myself that it's solid. That this is all real, even though it's crazy. Some people are at the base of this building, trying to get in. Hammering at the door. Who do they think is going to answer?

I wait for them to leave and then I go, too. Close my eyes and hurtle my body forward. Trusting that it's going to know what to do.

X, says the guidance counsellor, have you put in your applications yet?

I shrug. I'm sitting in her office for some kind of mandatory check in. I'm slumped in the green vinyl chair across the desk from her. There's a crack in the seat, and a pen lid someone has stuffed into it jams into my thigh. I leave it there, though. It seems wrong to move it. I push it farther into the foam while she watches me. She's the kind of person I always imagined as a mother. Not *my* mother, but like a sitcom mother. A TV mother. You know. Pretty. Together. Wears a suit to work. Lipstick. She looks like someone's mother from a 1950s movie or something. Stern, but loving. Normal.

Not quite real.

Not yet, I tell her.

Well, you know, Xenos, she says. You still have time.

She pronounces my name so long that it sounds like ZeeeeNose.

I know, I say. I just don't know where I want to go. I was thinking of a golf scholarship, maybe.

Were you? she says. I don't know whether you've got the grades for it, frankly. And what about your arm?

Oh, I say. I don't know. My arm will be fine. When it heals. Maybe I could go to college around here.

Ah, she says. Is it because you're worried about your family? I know you have a single mother and a little sister, is that right?

Brother, I say. I don't know. I just don't know what I want to do. I shrug again.

I want to give her the right answers, I do. I just don't know what the right answers are. And it all feels out of my control, like if I decide I want to golf, what if I can't? What if my arm doesn't heal right? What else am I good at? What if that option is gone?

What if I can't play anymore?

Ever?

I'll try to fill some applications out this weekend, I say, chewing on the end of my pencil, eraser bits clinging to my teeth. Pretending not to care. I spit out the rubbery plastic onto my hand, wipe my hand on my pants.

Well, she says. Let me know if you want me to look them over before you send them.

Sure, I say. Thanks.

Then that's that. I don't feel any more guided than I did when I walked in the door.

I look around for Tic and Robbo. Cat. Or anyone. I hate spending lunch alone. My arm is wickedly itchy. I feel like smashing it against the door frame, splitting the cast off and just scratching it raw. I settle for banging it against a locker, which hurts like hell. I scuff my shoes miserably as I wander through the halls. Nothing is going my way, I think. I feel pretty fucking sorry for myself, if you must know. Just when I think it can't get any worse, I see Tic and Cat disappearing down the basement stairs.

Great, I think. That's just fucking perfect.

I don't know how I get through the rest of the day, but I do.

I see you sitting in the library after school when I go in to return some computer stuff. Your head is bent down over a book and your hair looks greasy. Like you haven't washed it. You still look good, you just look ... sad. And it's everything I can do not to go over to you and to find out what's wrong. I'd do it if I didn't think you'd look at me like I was crazy. Or get up and leave. You know, sometimes I really just wish we were *friends*. Weird, huh. It's just that my friends are Tic and Robbo, and you know what they're like. They're buddies. Buds. Not real friends, not "Hey, I need a kidney, can you give me one?" friends. Not friends who actually want to see you cry, unless it's some kind of fucking joke and they can laugh with you about it.

And I have Cat. But for some reason, I just don't feel like Cat is a really good friend of mine right now.

I drop the stuff on the library counter hard so it makes a sound and you look up at me, just for a second, but I don't meet your eye. I turn and leave, letting the heavy door slam behind me.

I go home. I don't fly, I walk.

The driving range is completely deserted.

Week before Christmas, Bob says, sitting back in the deck chair he keeps out there all year around. He's warming his hands over a cup of coffee. The steam rises and covers his face.

Yeah, I say. I've got an iron out of my bag and I'm practising swinging with my left arm, my right arm just hanging there like a bag of flour or something. Useless.

You done your Christmas shopping? he says.

Sure, I say. Well, no.

To tell you the truth, I haven't even thought about it yet. Who do I need to buy presents for? Mutt, for sure. I've already decided that I'm going to get him some golf clubs, cut down to fit him. Hey, it's never too soon to start. And that way, maybe he can be good at it in a way that I'm not. Maybe Deer will switch her attention to him. Maybe he can make her dreams come true. I don't know what to get Deer. A signed picture of Tiger Woods would be a good bet, but I wouldn't be able to find one in this town. I'll probably get her perfume. Some of that patchouli shit that she likes so much even though the smell of it gives me a headache. I should get Cat something, I guess. She is still my girlfriend as far as I know. I knock a ball onto the mat and slice it sharply with my one-armed swing.

Shit, I say out loud. I suck at this.

It's harder than it looks, Bob says, lumbering up to his feet. He takes the iron from me, places a ball and hits it solidly with his left hand, right hand behind his back. It's a perfect shot. Pure.

But it's also a mental game, he winks, tapping his head. All up here, son.

No wonder I suck at it, then, I say.

It's hard to be seventeen, he says.

Not really, I say.

I remember, he says.

And I'm afraid he's going to start telling me a story from his past, blah blah blah, that will turn me around.

Will make everything okay. Seriously, sometimes Bob's stories are like Disney movies of the week, and about as long.

Hey, show me how to hit the shot, I say.

So he does. He loves that shit. I get a little better at it by the time the night is out. I shut the place up and fly home. Man, that sounds crazy, but it's true.

I'm getting careless. I guess it's just a matter of time before I get caught. Before I get turned into a joke or a laughingstock.

Or before it just stops altogether.

14

IT ISN'T UNTIL Cat is getting dressed for the Christmas dance that she realizes her period is late. Oh fuck, she says. Fuck, fuck, fuck, fuck. Of course. So stupid. So obvious.

She leaves her dress unzipped and goes into Mira's room and sits on Mira's bed.

I'm pregnant, she says.

If Mira were actually at home, instead of out with Perfect Nathan, Cat imagines that she would know what to do. But she isn't home. She's never home any more. You'd think she and Nathan were engaged the way they carry on. They only just met, after all. It drives Cat crazy.

She stands up and inspects her belly in the mirror. It looks the same. But all that throwing up. Sore breasts. No period. There's no mistake. She's as sure of this as she ever has been sure about anything. X's *baby*. A real baby, with eyes, nose, mouth. Unimaginable, really. When she tries to picture it, she can only picture babies she's seen in the mall or on TV or in movies or magazines. She guesses it would be a beautiful child. Why not? They are both okay-looking people. But still, it's not real.

It doesn't exist.

For a few minutes, she sits there, with her dress half hanging off, just forcing herself to imagine it. But she can't have it. She knows that. How can she? Why would she?

How can she not?

You ready yet? her mum calls up the stairs.

Just a minute, yells Cat. She looks at her reflection. The tight black dress looks like shit, she decides. She looks like a hooker, a fat bloated hooker stuffed into something too small. Gross. She goes over to Mira's closet and starts looking through her stuff, all of it shimmering with the smell of good cleanness, of Mira. She and Mira haven't shared clothes for years, but Mira wouldn't mind, or if she would, then fuck her.

Who cares? Who cares about anything? What does anything matter, when it comes down to it? Cat's thoughts are buzzing. She feels high and angry and low and dead at the same time. Her hands are shaking.

Oh my God, oh my God, she says.

She pulls out a skirt and a matching sparkly top. Sleeveless. It's pretty. Summery, but who cares? A pale mauve colour that makes her skin look even whiter and makes her eyes look almost purple. Perfect. She puts that on instead. And a pair of high-heeled silver sandals. Combs her hair. Uses her sister's makeup. Then, at the last minute, she pops out her facial piercings and drops them on her sister's dresser. Slicks her hair back smooth and ties the long bits up at the back so it looks like it's all on purpose, the style, the cut, the missing pieces.

Just for one night, she says to herself. Takes a deep breath and goes downstairs where her mum is waiting to drive her over to the dance. She's not allowed to drive anywhere any more.

Wow, says her mum. You look ... great.

It's Mira's, says Cat scathingly. We're twins, you know. What you're saying is that I look like Mira.

No, says her mum. You look great. *Bella*. My beautiful girl. I hope you aren't too cold in that though.

Yeah, whatever, says Cat. Thanks. Can we go now?

In the car, her mother tries again, You know, she says, if there is anything you want to talk about ...

Like what, mum? says Cat. The birds and the bees?

If only you knew, she thinks darkly. The lasagna she had for dinner is turning in her stomach, heavy and sharp, like she's swallowed a glass bottle and it's starting to crack. She almost asks her mum to stop the car so she can throw up, but then she doesn't. Instead, she coughs into her hand. Swallows hard. Gags.

I hope you don't think you're going to be drinking tonight, says her mum.

I'm *not*, says Cat. Don't worry.

Is X meeting you there?

Yeah, says Cat. I guess.

She thinks about it. He did say he was going, she was sure he said it. She just figured that meant they'd be going together. They are still a couple, sort of. Apart from that stupid thing with Tic that was meaningless, and X doesn't know about that. She sighs. Why can't anything be easy? She rests her hand on her belly. Sorry, baby, she says to herself.

What? says her mother, looking at her sharply.

Nothing, Ma, says Cat. Impetuously, she leans over and kisses her mum on the cheek. I'll see you at midnight.

Don't be late, says her mum. Have fun.

Yeah, says Cat. Fun.

The gym is full when she walks in. Everyone all decked out and stupid looking red and green streamers everywhere. A big tree in the middle decorated with coloured lights from the seventies. The music is so loud and the acoustics so bad that it just sounds like white noise. She glares at a few people who look at her and do double takes. Whispering to each other. About her, no doubt. She should have left her brow piercing in, at least. She needs a drink. Where are Tic and Robbo? She frowns. They're probably outside somewhere. Or in the basement. Somehow Tic got hold of a key. She pushes through the crowd and wanders down the hall toward the basement door. She's almost there, when someone calls her name. She turns.

Uh, Mr. Beardsley, hi, she says. I was just ...

You know you aren't supposed to be in this part of the school, he says.

Yeah, she improvises. I just wanted to get some, uh, a brush, to comb my hair. From my locker.

You look great, he says.

He's staring at her chest when he says it. He makes her so uncomfortable she just wants to run.

Thanks, she says. Well, I'll just be getting back to the ...

You know, he says. I've got a bottle of whiskey in my drawer. You could come into the classroom for a drink if you want.

Uh, she says. Aware that she's backing up while she's talking. I don't think ... I mean ...

Forget it, he says abruptly.

I just ... she says. Oh, fuck, Cat, she thinks. You're blowing it. But suddenly the whole flirting-with-a-teacher thing seems like a really bad idea. I'm not ... she says.

Never mind, little girl, he says.

She never noticed before how he squinted when he talked. How mean he looked. How old he looked.

Look, I'm not feeling well, she says. She darts around him and runs into the girls' washroom. She isn't feeling well. It takes her a few minutes to throw up the lasagna. It spatters the front of her pale purple top.

Shit, she says, trying to scrub it off, looking in the mirror.

I can help with that, I have these stain things, a voice says behind her.

She whirls around, startled. It's just Ruby. Eerie Ruby with the big dark eyes. She looks nervous.

Thanks, says Cat, grabbing the stain remover and dabbing at her shirt. Bad lasagna.

Are you okay? says Ruby.

Yeah, says Cat. I'm in the peak of health.

I just thought I heard you ...

I threw up, okay? says Cat. It happens.

Well, as long as ...

I'm pregnant, says Cat before she can stop herself.

The other girl is staring at her in the mirror. They are both facing forward. This strikes Cat as odd, but she doesn't turn her head.

Oh, says Ruby. That's ...

It sucks, says Cat. I don't know what I'm going to do.

Oh God, says Ruby. I'm sorry.

Yeah, says Cat. Listen, some of us are having a drink downstairs, why don't you come? Just don't say anything.

I won't, says Ruby.

Not that you can't talk at all, says Cat hurriedly. I mean, you can talk. Just don't mention this, if that's okay.

Yeah, says Ruby. Totally.

The basement is cold and unheated tonight. And dark. Instead of turning the lights on, they've lit candles, some of them scented, and the air is cloying and sweet. It looks spooky.

It's like *Buffy the Vampire Slayer* down here, says Cat. She shouts, Hey, are you losers down here?

Boo, says Robbo, jumping out in a costume from the rack.

Fuck, says Cat. You scared me, you asshole.

Who are you? says Robbo, shining his flashlight into Ruby's face.

It's me, Ruby, says Ruby.

Oh, says Robbo. Come and have a drink.

Ruby, says Tic quietly. Cat notices a look pass between them. Oh, great, she thinks. It's like a little love triangle.

Where's X? Cat says, swallowing from the bottle that someone passes her. It crashes into her empty stomach and makes her nearly gag again. It's sweet and horrible.

What the hell is that? she says. It's awful.

It's alcohol, says Tic. Don't complain. He nudges her and she leans into him.

Ruby doesn't say anything. She just sits there, playing with her hair. Cat almost feels like asking her what she's doing there, but then she remembers that she invited her.

Have a drink, she says, dropping the bottle into Ruby's hand.

Thanks, says Ruby. She sips it politely.

You remind me of my sister, says Cat.

Uh, thanks, says Ruby.

Yeah, says Cat. It isn't much of a compliment. Listen, I gotta go find X.

He'll come down here when he gets here, says Tic.

I don't care, says Cat. I want to find him. I'll be back.

She just feels itchy. Like she has to move around. The alcohol has warmed her up from the inside, and she can feel a flush on her cheeks. She almost feels like she can tell X. That she'll tell him and he'll help her. He'll figure it out. He'll save her. Right?

She sneaks out of the basement carefully, leaving the other three to get drunk or do whatever they are going to do. She doesn't even care. Back in the crowded gym, she sifts through the crowd with her eyes. Usually X is easy to spot, what with the fact that he's head and shoulders taller than everyone else. Not here. She sighs in frustration. Shakes her head when some boy she doesn't recognize asks her to dance.

Come on, he says.

No thanks, loser, she says. She may not be pierced tonight, but she suddenly feels more dangerous than ever. More crazy. Like maybe tonight is her last chance to do something wild. She pushes her fingers through her hair and tucks it behind her ears. Where are you, X? she says, even though no one can hear her over the driving beat of the music. The music seems to sort of seep into her and to take over from her heart. It beats in her blood. She can feel her arms and legs vibrating. For a minute, she dances with herself. Then she steps away from the dance floor again and goes to wait for X by the front door. She wants to see him when he walks in. She wants him to see her.

She wants him to see how she isn't waiting. How she's dancing and sweaty and drunk already and not needing him.

She wants him to ...

She doesn't know what she wants.

She waits for ages, but he doesn't come. An hour goes by, and then another. She hates to wait. I'm going to tell him and then I'm going to dump him, she thinks cruelly. She wants him to be upset. She almost wants to make him cry. She slumps back against the wall and slides into a sitting position. She has all the time in the world. She can wait.

Ruby

15

YOU NEVER HAVE liked being in enclosed spaces where there are candles. Candles remind you of the fire.

Sure, you were three.

Yeah, you're over it. (Although, do you ever get over something like that?)

But being in the basement with the flickering candles is making you afraid. You drink more than you normally would. You swallow whatever is in the bottle like it can save you. It doesn't take long for you to feel drunk. You didn't eat much dinner before you came out. Cassidy was there, like Cassidy is always there. Prattling on over salad about the golf clubs that your dad bought her as an early Christmas gift. She's crazy about golf. Your dad even took you out for a "lesson." As soon as you figured out why he wanted you to learn, you put your foot down. Told him you hated golf. Told him you'd never go again.

Want me to braid your hair for you? Cassidy had asked.

No, you'd said.

No, thank you, said your dad.

I wasn't offering to braid *your* hair, darling, Cassidy had said and then laughed like she was the funniest person alive.

That's hilarious, you'd said flatly, rearranging your fish on your plate and tucking some beans underneath it.

Why aren't you eating? your father asked.

No reason, you said. Nervous, I guess.

Well, that's normal, he said.

Yeah, you said. I know. It's just a dance. I'm not really nervous. I just said that.

I love dancing, said Cassidy.

Well, we don't do much dancing, you said. It's not like a real dance. It's just everyone dressed up making out with each other.

Sounds ... fun, said Cassidy.

You glared at her and pushed your chair back from the table. I've got to get ready, you said. The truth was, you were starving. There was just something about Cassidy and the way she kept touching your father's hand that made a lump rise in your throat. It was hard to swallow past it.

And now here you are. Swallowing and swallowing. Tic and Robbo aren't exactly great conversationalists. It's pretty much just drinking.

Hey, Joey, you say.

Yeah, he says. No one calls me that.

I know, you say. I just wanted to ask you something.

Yeah, he says. What?

But before you can ask, he says, Cat looks so hot tonight. I wish she'd just dump X so I can take a crack at her.

Which stops you cold. You can't ask him now. Even fuelled by alcohol.

Oh, you say. I ...

You almost tell him. For a split second, you almost want to say, She's pregnant. But something stops you. You don't have a lot of friends, after all. Maybe Cat will be the one friend that you remember from high school. No one remembers their high school friends. Your dad told you that. He told you none of it was as important as it seemed.

My dad says, you start. Then you stop. Tic and Robbo don't care. They're just jackasses. Jackasses you've known for a long time, but still jackasses. It occurs to you that you and Joey have never really had a good conversation, not the kind where you both get to talk and you both try to understand each other. It's mostly just been you listening and him getting high and talking and puking and letting you watch.

I've got to go find my friends, you say, getting to your feet.

Don't leave, says Robbo in a tone that means "leave already."

Whatever, you say. Catch you later.

You stumble a bit on the stairs and have to pause for a minute to get oriented. I'm drunk, you think. You've never been drunk. It's kind of funny. You start to laugh, but it echoes in the hallway, so you stop. You try to walk normally. In a weird way, you feel like everyone is looking at you. You keep your eyes on the blood-red linoleum.

Blood-red, you whisper. For a second, you think you're going to faint. Fade to black, you say out loud. And you laugh. Shh, you say, you're embarrassing yourself.

You duck into the washroom and splash cold water on your face. Your cheeks are bright red, not to mention your nose. You drink deeply from the faucet, not caring about the germs for once. You actually feel pretty good. Surprising. You don't look that good, but who cares? There's no one here to impress. Fuck you, Joey, you say to the mirror.

You have a weird feeling in the pit of your stomach. Like you're going to throw up, but different. More like a feeling of ... you don't know. You can't explain it, so it's a good thing you don't have to try. You head back toward the gym, trying not to stumble and give yourself away. For some reason, you think that if you can get to the music, you'll be all right. Like it can somehow prop you up. You stumble past the front door and you see Cat sitting there, but you don't stop. You don't even acknowledge her. The music is pulling you too loudly.

When you get to the gym, you feel like you can finally breathe. Even though there is a crush of people and they all seem to be pressing up against you. It makes you feel safe. You step out onto the dance floor and start swaying to the song. This is okay, you think. I'm okay.

You don't know how long you are there for, dancing by yourself. It seems like forever and it seems like only a few minutes. You are still dancing — well, swaying, anyway — when the fire alarms start to go off and the music stops. It takes you forever to recognize that it's not part of the song. It takes even longer for you to realize what it means.

Fade to black, you say, and then you faint. Rush of blood to your ears, drowning out everything else. Grey spots spreading so fast to cover everything, nothing. Your head hitting the gym floor so hard as all around you students rush, fall, trip, stampede to get out of the building. To escape.

X

16

I DIDN'T EVEN want to come to this dance. Fuck it. It's going to be a disaster. I'm pretty sure Cat is going to dump me for real, or maybe she and Tic will just show up together, which would be worse. Humiliating. My jaw hurts from clenching.

I'm wearing a suit I borrowed from one of the other guys at the golf course. It's too short in the legs, so I look like the kind of idiot I'd normally laugh at. I shouldn't have come. I don't want to be here. Everything feels wrong about it, my skin feels too tight or too loose. The air isn't going right into my lungs.

I stand outside the dance for a long time. Breathing fresh cool air. Trying to get over myself. The gym is throbbing with music. I have no desire to go in. Instead, I cut around back and I go sit in the breezeway. There's a guy there, smoking, but it's not a kid. It's a teacher, Mr. Bored-off-My-Ass Beardsley.

Hi, I say, trying not to meet his eye.

Yeah, he says. I hate this school.

Me too, I say.

He doesn't look inclined to say anything else, so I turn my back on him. I'm relieved. I don't want to talk to him. Or anyone for that matter. Anyway, he looks a little whacked out, to tell you the truth. Or a little drunk. He's such a loser. Such an insipid, pointless guy, like a human slug, heavy and somehow untouchable. Tonight he looks ... crazed. Great, I think. It's the stuff that horror movies are made of. Maybe he'll go nuts and kill us all.

But maybe he actually just looks old and sad. And probably wasted.

What a jerk.

I sit there for a while, and then I get up and walk over to the track. I kind of jog around it. I don't know why I do that. It's cold and slippery and my shoes, which don't fit properly, slip on the patches of ice. I'm not a good runner at the best of times. I'm out of breath by the time I get to the farthest point from the school. That's okay though. It's really dark here, and the sky is like fucking velvet or something. It's really beautiful. It's a full moon, and it's below freezing, so the moon has that light halo it forms on really chilly nights. I stand there until my feet get so cold I can hardly take the pain. Weird how being cold hurts so much. It's stupid, I know, but I fly up to the roof of the gym. I don't know what I'm thinking. Anyone could see me. Mr. B. probably saw me for sure. I don't care.

I wish I had X-ray vision and then I could look through the roof at the dancers. See who's dancing with whom and all that. See Cat dancing with Tic, which is what I figure is happening. It feels shitty to be screwed over by a guy who's supposed to be your friend, but I don't care that much. What I really want to see is who you are dancing with. If you're dancing at all. If you're even here.

Man, I think, shivering. This is so fucked up. My arm aches more from the cold, like the ice has seeped into the crack in the bone and the bone is shivering under my skin. It's the kind of ache you want to get at, want to cut into so you can get closer to it and rub it away.

What am I doing up here? I used to be the guy who never even climbed a ladder because I'm afraid of heights. I don't understand what's happened to me, why it's all changed, who I'm turning into. I'm dangling my feet over the edge. If you were driving down the street, you'd see me. My shiny shoes are right over the second S in the sign that says SECONDARY SCHOOL. You'd think, Look at that asshole, there's an accident waiting to happen.

But I'm not really, am I? An accident waiting to happen, I mean. I'm probably an asshole, sure. I'm pretty much accident proof now, I guess.

I'm the kid who can *fly*. I'm the kid who can save myself. It's like being immortal in a way, isn't it? I can't fall.

I lean forward and look down to see if I can even scare myself, but the thing is, I can't. I don't feel even slightly nervous. I just feel safe.

And more than a little bit cold.

I should go in, but I'm dreading the scene. Dreading the drama. Dreading seeing Cat. That's a different kind of pain. The kind of pain you can't just rub away.

I lie back and stare up at the stars and say, Well, God, what next then? Or Goddess? To tell you the truth, I don't know what I believe as far as God and all that goes. I used to not believe in anything. Nothing.

But what the fuck? I can fly, I have to believe that something caused that to happen. That didn't just *happen*. I just don't know what it is.

Magic, maybe.

Myself.

But that's so fucked up — it's like a joke — because while I no longer think that I can ever fall, I don't believe in myself at all. That's why I'm such a crappy golfer, if you must know. Technically, I'm good. I may even be great. I know I am. But when I'm up there on the tee and everyone is staring at me and expecting me to make the drive, expecting the magic of Tiger Woods? That's when I choke. I don't believe I can do it. I don't believe I can meet their expectations. Or my own.

That's the real truth. And now I'll probably never get a chance to try. I look at my arm. Deer and Mutt decorated it for me for the dance. It's covered with glitter, which is mostly all over my suit. There's red and green holly. And Deer has written MERRY CHRISTMAS, but upside down, so that it looks the right way up to me when I look down.

As I was leaving, she grabbed me and said, Promise me you'll be careful.

I said, Yeah, sure.

I kissed Mutty goodbye.

Be careful? It's just a dance, after all. What could possibly go wrong?

I'm just about to go down and face the music when the fire alarm goes off. At first, I think it's a joke. I mean, there is always some asshole who pulls the alarm thing at a dance. Invariably it's Tic. Or Rocco. Probably on a dare, or whatever. Just to be a jerk. So I don't think much of it until people start streaming out of the school. Running.

Panicking. Now I'm really fucked, I think, pulling my legs up and backing up so they can't see me. I mean, I can't exactly fly down there in front of all those people, can I?

No.

Of course not.

The smoke smell hits me then. The cinder-burning smell of something terrible.

I hide. Because I'm a big fucking hero, shivering behind the air conditioning ducts on the roof of the school while it burns underneath me.

I told you I was a jerk, right? So you can't be surprised by this. I close my eyes, too. I can hear people shouting, and in the distance, the sirens approach. Even as I see the flashing lights, I start to see smoke curling up from the vents. It can't be happening, I think. It isn't real. Just like the flying thing isn't real. It's just some kind of fucked-up hallucination.

Then I think of you. And I think, Oh, no.

Ruby.

Fire.

17

AS SOON AS the fire alarm starts to sound, Cat leaps to her feet, her heart pounding like crazy. In her mind's eye, she sees the candles. Tic, she thinks. Oh, fuck, no. She runs against the flow of people who are all pushing to get out. Runs toward the basement and manages to get the door open. It's full of smoke. Of course it is. She's yelling, Tic Tic Tic and she's choking on the smoke and she can't see, and that's when she trips and falls. It's not like the last time that she fell.

This time, no one catches her. Her body falls hard on the stairs, landing impossibly twisted on the basement floor. Between racks of burning clothes. Beside boxes that are just beginning to ignite.

Cat, someone yells, but she doesn't know who, or maybe she's just imagined it. She's floating and falling and what is she doing? She's landing, but she's not. She's up and down and dizzy and falling.

Falling.

And then she stops hearing anything at all. Because she's not conscious any more. She's left her body. She's up somewhere near the stars, where there is a cold halo around the moon, where the air is clean and breathable.

She's gone.

Blood spreads in a widening pool on Mira's pretty mauve skirt.

Ruby

18

You are gone. Checked out. Faded to black. Around you, the gym is empty but rapidly filling with smoke. It's coming from the basement, but you don't know that. It's just everywhere at once. In your lungs. Touching your skin.

Outside, the firemen have arrived and are bursting through the front door with hoses and masks. But you don't hear them. You aren't there.

Someone told you once that people who are unconscious don't dream, but that can't be true. Because you are dreaming now. You are having a dream that X is there. You are dreaming that he is picking you up and that he is carrying you up toward the ceiling. You are dreaming that you are lying on the roof of the burning school and that X is sitting next to you saying, Please wake up, Ruby, please wake up, oh shit oh shit oh shit.

X

19

PLEASE WAKE UP, Ruby, I say again.

I'm shaking you. I know I shouldn't. I don't want you to be dead.

Is this it? I ask out loud. Was *this* what I was supposed to do?

But if I wanted to save you, I shouldn't have brought you up here. I can't get you down. I don't know what happened, but once we landed here, I couldn't do it any more. I don't know what to do. I'm so fucked. One day, they'll make a fucking comic book of this and I'll be, like, the anti-hero. So far, I've done two things. One of them crippled me, and now I've saved you but only temporarily. If the school burns down, we'll go down with it.

I stand up and rock back on my heels. Come on, I say to myself. Just do it.

But I can't. What if I fuck it up? This isn't something I can mess up and still be able to live with myself. You know? This is so important. It's the most important. It's the only thing that matters.

You.

Please wake up, I say.

And you do. You look at me with wild, red eyes. Your breath is sweet, like you've been drinking. You say, What am I doing on the roof?

I try to explain, about the fire, but you just stare off into the sky. You say, I have dreams like this, full of fire. Everyone always dies. Melts. You know?

I nod and say, I know. I want to take you in my arms, but I'm not that suave. I can't pull it off. This isn't a Hollywood movie. If it was, I would have soared with you in my arms down to the ground. I would have saved you like a man, like Superman. Instead of waiting here helplessly, broken-armed, cowardly and useless. It's like now you're awake, I can't do it. Getting you up here, hanging over my cast, holding you tight with my good arm was one thing when you were unconscious. But now? Well, now you'd see.

You'd *know*.

I want you to know. I guess I do. I just can't move. I can't lift you. I don't know how to start. I'm thinking too much. My heart is beating as though handfuls of pebbles are being tossed around in my chest. Scattershot.

I should just *do* it. Do it. But I can't. It's like a bad dream where you know you have to run but your feet are stuck to the floor and moving isn't an option. The air is too heavy to pass through. The night is too dense to carry us up. Or down.

There is the sound of breaking glass. People shouting.

I guess we should call for help, you say. And for a second, I almost laugh. I didn't think of that. I'm so stupid.

We go over to the edge and start shouting. Me and you. And they see us, of course they do. I'm sure later they'll ask how the hell we got up here and we'll have to lie or explain somehow; I have no fucking idea how. In the meantime, I stand on the roof with you and hold your hand in my good hand and we wait for them to rescue us.

And you know something, holding your hand is the best thing that's ever happened to me. But then it's ruined, because you turn to me and you say, I'm drunk.

I know, I say. It's okay.

Cat's pregnant, you say. I feel like I'm the one who's falling this time. It's like the roof drops away from behind me.

What? I say.

You heard me, she says. I don't know why I'm telling you.

Just then, a couple of firemen appear. I guess they came up on a ladder. I don't know why I didn't look. Oh, yeah, because I'm stupid, that's right. They kind of push us down between them and we have to go and I'm just reeling and the school is exploding in front of me and it's the most surreal thing ever, you holding my hand and the gas in the science labs blowing up and no sign of Cat anywhere in the crowd and no one knows where she is and I feel like I'm broken inside and I'll never ever be okay again.

20

THE FIREMEN STRAP you to the body board and lift you. You're only vaguely aware of it. You can breathe. There is something over your nose and lips. There is blood all over you. You can't tell where it is coming from. It's warm and sticky. You feel like you'll be okay, though. The flames are almost pretty.

I'm okay, you try to say, but you can't talk because there is a tube in your nose. You're so sleepy it's hard to stay awake. Hard to concentrate on the way they lift you out and run down the hall, with you jostling up and down, and your locker passing by, and an explosion behind you that propels you out of the building and somehow you are in an ambulance and you are ...

Ruby

21

YOU WATCH THE school burn, from a safe distance. The flames are unfamiliar to you, like you've never seen fire before. They seem too colourless to be real. After all, in your dreams they were always so orange.

So colourful.

So bright.

You feel sick from drinking and from the smoke, and your body is bruised and battered from people stepping on you while they were trying to escape.

No one is dead, right? you ask, but no one answers you. No one knows anything. It's freezing outside, but except for the people who are carried away in ambulances, no one is going anywhere. You all just stand there and watch the school burn, colourless flames licking the sky like a thirsty dog, like a million thirsty dogs. Parched. Desperate.

It feels like the end of the world. You think, Nothing else matters. You think, This is the second time I've survived it, that has to mean something. You think, I'm immortal. Maybe nothing can kill me.

X stands next to you. He's crying. He seems to be holding your hand and that feels okay. They took Cat off in an ambulance. She was covered with blood and soot and she was unconscious. You don't know what to think.

You hear later that she lost the baby. The baby that no one knew about except you. And X, because you told him.

You hear that Cat switched schools, she won't come back to this one even when it's rebuilt. You hear that she's pressing sexual harassment charges against Mr. B. It's all too much, you think, but then you realize that it isn't. It's over, and you survived. You feel better than you've ever felt. It's weird, but it's true.

You don't know who to tell about that, so you call X. You tell him that.

And he says, I have something for you to read.

DON'T MISS THE NEXT AMAZING
TITLE IN THE XYZ TRILOGY...

Y in the Shadows

"I DON'T WANT to disappear. But also, I do."

Quick quick quick as anything, before I can think about how to do it or why I'm doing it, I do It. I make myself disappear. In an instant, a heartbeat. Fade, fade, fade. *He can't see me watching him*, I think. *Too awkward. Stalkerish.* Go, go, go.

Almost gone.

If he saw me, I would die. Just like those silly, overly dramatic girls that I'm not. I would *die*. I'm too gross. He would be embarrassed to see me.

How else could he feel, being watched by ... the-girl-with-the-weird-eyes? I'm sure that's all he knows me as. He wouldn't know me for any other reason.

I almost have to concentrate on staying faded, it's like I'm thinking it without being able to stop myself, getting darker, then lighter, then lighter still. It's the sleepiness somehow interfering with the idea.

And I'm completely gone, shimmering. It feels like hard work, like my skull is too tight. My hair follicles too hot. Too cold. Both.

Without warning, the bum staggers to his feet and runs toward me. He's staring right at me. He claps. Laughing. Well, not laughing so much as grimacing and making a choking sound. Toppling.

"Are you all right?" It's Tony, approaching. I'm so close I can touch him but he can't see me.

I'm right *here*.

I'm not completely gone ... Sort of like a shadow ...

I'm aware that I feel papery and thin ...

I feel like I can't possibly stay on the ground, like I'll float away.

I clear my throat, but no sound comes out. Interesting. I'm mute. So I don't just vanish, I'm silenced as well. I say, "Tony." And he doesn't react.

What am I?

What is happening to me?

THE XYZ TRILOGY
by Karen Rivers

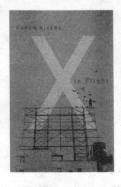  

Artwork subject to change

Author's Note

Did you know that when the term "hero" was coined, it referred only to men? Crazy, don't you think? Now that's all changed. Everyone can be a hero. Everyone. And at the risk of sounding like a PSA, this includes you. And me. And that obnoxious kid who sits next to you in Biology. Heroism isn't just something for rich people to do or for people with a lot of spare time or for celebrities or for people who randomly discover that they can fly. It's for all of us. And if every single person performs one small yet heroic task, think how much better things will be.

Being a hero is the one thing you'll do in your life that you'll never regret. And it's never too late or too early to do something that can change someone else's life. It's so easy! It's ridiculously easy! I'm not saying you have to save kittens from burning buildings or anything like that. Just get a bit involved or even just give an hour or two of your time. Donate some blood. Be an organ donor. Support a charity. Or just give a hand to someone who looks like they need it.

There's so much going on in the world right now that picking a cause can be overwhelming. Just pick something and go for it. I'll have some links to some great charities and causes posted on my website, www.karenrivers.com.

Life is full of choices; you can choose to be someone extraordinary for someone else. And I hope that you will.

Thanks for listening.